BUYING
THE
BUSINESS

BUYING
THE
BUSINESS

Bertram Henry

HUTCHINSON
London Sydney Auckland Johannesburg

This edition first published in 1990 by Hutchinson

Century Hutchinson Ltd, Brookmount House,
20 Vauxhall Bridge Road, London SW1V 2SA

Century Hutchinson Australia (Pty) Ltd
20 Alfred Street, Milsons Point
Sydney NSW 2061, Australia

Century Hutchinson New Zealand Limited
PO Box 40–086, Glenfield, Auckland 10, New Zealand

Century Hutchinson South Africa (Pty) Ltd
PO Box 337, Bergvlei, 2012 South Africa

British Library Cataloguing in Publication Data

Henry, Bertram
  Buying thr business.
  I. Title
  823'.914   [F]

ISBN 0-09-174358-3

Set in Baskerville by 🅐 Tek Art Ltd. Croydon, Surrey
Printed and bound in Great Britain by
The Guernsey Press Co. Ltd., Guernsey, Channel Islands.

For Cissie

There is no den in the wide world to hide a rogue. Commit a crime and the earth is made of glass.

Ralph Waldo Emerson

Nonsense!

Nicos Papadopoulos

'Tis pleasant purchasing our fellow-creatures;
And all are to be sold if you consider
Their passions, and are dext'rous; some by features
Are brought up, others by a warlike leader;
Some by a place – as tend their years or natures;
The most by ready cash – but all have prices,
From crowns to kicks, according to their vices.

Lord Byron

Now you're talking!

Nicos Papadopoulos

CHAPTER
1

Singapore twinkled and glowed as the aircraft came in over the South China Sea, losing height over the great harbour dotted with pinpoint lights from the armada of vessels anchored random-fashion in the glassy waters. George looked down on the lights of the city, picking out the roads and landmarks he knew and sensing the familiar touch of excitement and expectation that he always got from the place. 'I know it's something of a con,' he told himself. 'In fact, it's a cultural monstrosity, a Western city run by Easterners and run better than we can do it now in the West. It's also the ultimate tourist trap. They lure them here by the millions and really there's nothing to do but buy Jap and Korean imports and gawp at the housing estates. I know all that, but I still get a kick out of it.'

Perhaps the moment he liked best was when the doors of the aircraft had been switched to manual and the steward had pulled his levers and at last let a wave of unprocessed local air into the air-conditioned cabin. With it came the background noises of jet engines on the runways, the evocative odour of paraffin, and in the foreground, the clipped Chinese-inflected English of the ground staff at the top of the gangway. And walking out onto the steps amid 'goodbyes' and 'thank-yous' was always like walking into the outer room of a Turkish bath. The hot, humid air enfolded one like a medium lying somewhere between real air and warm bath water, and one wondered briefly how one could ever stand this climate. Then the white-uniformed and businesslike health and immigration staff, and on to the baggage hall to await his bag.

Back behind the glass barrier he could see the smiling

and subtle features of Mr Sombolon and next to him Sandy Macarthur, blond and cool in a pale blue safari suit of immaculate local cut. George Pidduck waved and they waved back. He was stiff from the eighteen-hour journey and a little muzzy from the passage through so many time zones.

Soon he had his bag and was shaking Sandy and Mr Sombolon by the hand.

'We are deeply honoured,' Mr Sombolon said. 'Much happiness is caused.'

'Thanks, Mr Sombolon,' George Pidduck said. 'How's the family?'

'My wife is honoured that you ask. She is pretty damn well, I fear. The children are perhaps well also.'

George Pidduck did not follow up this enigmatic reply. They picked their way through the crowds, out into the steamy heat of the car park and to Sandy's car. As the driver forced his way through the heavy evening traffic towards the city, he checked the arrangements.

'Where have you booked me?'

'The Shangri-La, Mr Pidduck.'

'Good. When do we move on to Jakarta?'

'I have a wonderful influence at the Indonesian Embassy here,' Mr Sombolon said. 'You will honour them with your visit tomorrow morning to see my good friend Mr Dipa Supit, who may grant you rapidly a visa. It is not expensive.' Mr Sombolon always tried to price everything that he proposed. 'Maybe twenty dollars.'

'*May* grant my visa? Is that the best you've been able to do, Mr Sombolon?'

'If my friend Mr Dipa Supit admires you, he will certainly grant you a very good visa. Also cheap.'

'Does that mean we can get out of here tomorrow?'

'Undoubtedly.'

'If your friend admires me enough.'

'Of course. But we can ensure admiration. It is not very expensive at all.'

'And what about flight tickets?'

'I have also wonderful influence at Garuda airline.

There will be no problem.'

'I don't want to fly Garuda.'

'Then I have no influence any more. All seats will certainly be occupied for many days. That is my information.'

'From KLM and Singapore Airlines?'

'From Garuda.'

Pidduck grunted, too tired to pursue with Mr Sombolon the intricacies of airline reservations. 'We'll wait till tomorrow to talk about the General. I need some shut-eye first.'

They took their leave in the hotel's vast lobby, Sandy Macarthur to return to his villa in Tanglin, and Mr Sombolon to continue downtown to an obscure corner of the old city favoured by Indonesian families. These were immigrants who had fled successive waves of ideological mayhem in their native country – by the Dutch colonial authorities against the evils of socialism, by Sokarno against the evils of capitalism, by Suharto ingeniously and confusingly against both. Here Mr Sombolon had family.

'Daphne.'

'Yes, my sweet?'

'Daphne, don't call me that in the office.'

'Yes, my . . . yes, Mr Pipe.'

'Daphne, what is this rubbish you've put among my mail?'

'Do you mean the cable for George Pidduck?

'I do.'

'Well, you'll see it says URGENCY TIPTOP. Rather quaint, I thought. And with Mr Pidduck out this afternoon, his secretary felt you ought to see it.'

'Did you understand it?'

'Me? Heavens, no.'

'Am I expected to understand it?'

'Search me.'

'I'll do that later.' Rufus Pipe sniggered into the telephone.

'Don't be vulgar,' Daphne said.

'When's George Pidduck expected in?'

'Tomorrow.'

'I suppose it'll hold till then. See that he gets it as soon as he arrives.'

'Yes, Mr Pipe, Sir.'

They both hung up.

The cable had been filed in Jakarta:

ALLOIL LONDON

ATTENTION MR GEORGE PIDDUCK SALES DIRECTOR

URGENCY TIPTOP

MILDRED UNBOUGHT FRENCHWISE REJECTS FORNICATION TRANSPORTATION ACCOMMODATION LUBRICATION IMPERATIVE YOU COME OTHERWISE BALLSUP ISNT IT MY HUMBLEST ADMIRATIONS AND GREETINGS SIR THANKYOU GLADYS

Rufus Pipe, Managing Director of All World Oil Services, shook his head and turned to an irritable letter from the Chairman of the National Oil Corporation of Guinea Bissau. He met the irritability of Mr E.E. Olufemi, Chairman of the NOCGB, with an equivalent exasperation of his own.

He was thinking of Daphne's exuberant sexuality. He picked up the handset of the intercom.

'Is tonight any good?'

''Fraid not. W'shing m'hair.'

'Can't you do that tomorrow?'

'N'nn. Going out t'morrow.' Her mouth appeared to be full.

'What are you eating?'

'A bun. You said I was skinny.'

'Never mind that. When can you manage?'

'Don't know right now.' There was a gulping sound. 'Let you know, though.'

'All right, but I hate waiting for you.' He hung up. He was, in the words of Daphne to her friend Sue, distracted with passion.

4

'And he's nothing to send postcards home about,' she added.

'They rarely are', Sue said. 'Not so's you'd notice, like.'

'Mr Pidduck is,' she said. 'He's fantastic.'

'Next morning George Pidduck was in Pipe's office.

'For Christ's sake explain that rigmarole,' Rufus Pipe said.

George Pidduck held the strange cable by a corner. The expression on his face was one of worry, verging on alarm.

'It's from Sombolon, our agent in Jakarta.'

'But it's signed Gladys.'

'That's the cover name I gave him. You can't be too careful. The Indonesians read everything.'

'It reads like a mix of cost-conscious cablese and expansive oriental flummery.'

'That's because everything Sombolon can ever need to tell me has been put into cable jargon for him, to ensure secrecy and economy. We lay that down. The rest of it is him making sure I'm flattered.'

'Who pays for these cables?'

'I'm afraid we do, Rufus, but the man's uncontrollable when it comes to licking backsides. If he sees one, he licks it. Part of the culture.'

Rufus Pipe snorted. 'Now tell me what it means.'

'As a matter of fact,' George Pidduck said, 'it's pretty damn serious. Look, I've punctuated it for a start.' He handed the cable across the desk. It now read:

MILDRED UNBOUGHT FRENCHWISE. REJECTS FORNICATION, TRANSPORTATION, ACCOMMODATION, LUBRICATION. IMPERATIVE YOU COME, OTHERWISE BALLS-UP, ISN'T IT. MY HUMBLEST ADMIRATIONS AND GREETINGS, SIR, THANK YOU. GLADYS.

'Before,' Pipe said, 'it was continuous rubbish. Now it's rubbish broken down into bits. You'll have to explain it to me.'

'Well,' George Pidduck said, 'Mildred is our code

name for General Nasturtion. As you'll remember, he's Chairman of Entakan. Then, "unbought Frenchwise" means our private arrangements with him have come unstuck. He was bought, you understand, but now he isn't. Unbought, see? And the French, of all people, have captured him for the new contract.'

'You mean they've bought him – paid more than we do?'

'That's what it says, though frankly I don't see what they could have offered that was more attractive than our own arrangements.'

'Go on.'

'Next, the cable tells us he's rejecting all the usual inducements. "Fornication" is the code word for women.'

'Not very subtle, that.'

'Maybe, but adequate for the purpose.'

'What's "transportation", for God's sake? Bicycles?'

'Rolls-Royces. Maybe Mercedes. Once it was a Lamborghini. Anyway, he's not responding to cars. He's got fourteen. Maybe fifteen.'

'I suppose "accommodation" is castles and palaces. The Vatican, perhaps?'

'Don't joke. He's already had a million dollar villa off us, at Cap Ferrat, and places in Switzerland and Mexico off the Americans. After all, he has to live somewhere when the country decides it can't afford him any more.'

'And "lubrication"?'

'Cash. Folding money, pure and simple. Seems he's rejecting that too.'

Rufus Pipe grunted. 'What, as they say, do you offer a man who has everything?'

'And much of it off you,' George added. 'A very good question. It keeps me awake nights. Whenever the Entakan contract comes up for renewal I go crazy thinking up what to offer him. In the end, of course, the General lets his wishes be known. Sometimes it's bloody difficult, at others bloody expensive, usually both together.'

6

'I don't want to know,' Pipe said. 'This company does not offer bribes or inducements, it being against the 1974 Act.'

'That's right,' George Pidduck said. 'We just facilitate the process. Lubrication, you see. The actual job's done by old Sombolon with humblest admirations. It's why I usually don't bother you with it.'

Pipe grunted again. 'What's the contract worth this time?'

'Well, there's the usual servicing of the rigs, a certain amount of new hardware, supplies of drilling mud and so on and so forth . . . around sixteen million dollars, all up. Plus what the General himself will cost. He's a very reasonable chap. Doesn't expect us to wreck our own margins to look after him. "I want your best price as gentlemen," he says. "I, too, am a gentleman. I will not rob you. I understand the need for healthy margins. No, you will simply add my modest service charge to your price." He reckons he's entitled to a reward for enabling us to do business with Entakan. "Without me you can sell nothing," he says, "so if I help you to sell to my Corporation, is that not a service and should it not be rewarded like any service?" Then he tells you what he wants. Last time it was five German blondes.'

'Bonds? What sort of bonds?'

'I didn't say bonds. I said blondes. Women. He even gave Sombolon the measurements. He's a wiry little runt, about 5ft 2ins. He's partial to solidly built German women. He specified 48-inch hips.'

'You mean to tell me you procured him five German women with big arses?'

'I don't like that word, Rufus.'

'What's wrong with arses?'

'Not arses. Procured. I don't like procured. But yes, we found 'em for him. Or rather, Sombolon did. I don't have anything to do with that sort of thing.'

Pipe shook his head. 'Do you mean to say, George, that this world-famous company of ours, quoted on the London, New York and Amsterdam exchanges and

7

second only to Brown & Root in its field, sells its goods and services on the basis of a common pimping operation?'

'I do mean to tell you that, Rufus, since you ask. Normally, you're smart enough not to ask. But since you're asking this time, yes, I'll do damn nearly anything to land my contracts, and I'll do it because the Japs and the Yanks will always do more if they get the chance. And just so long as I'm filling our order books and holding our margins I don't think you've any cause for complaint.'

'Just tell me one thing,' Pipe said. 'Did these German girls mind?'

'I've no idea,' George Pidduck said, reflectively, 'but if it interests you, I'll ask old Sombolon next time I see him.'

'Never mind,' Pipe said. 'What do you propose to do about the cable?'

'If Sombolon says come, it's because he can't swing it without me. The tenders are all in and opening date's the day after tomorrow. Not that that means much, since the whole thing's rigged and the tendering is just a neat oriental obeisance in the general direction of the law. But it's pretty clear that I'd better catch some sort of aeroplane tonight.'

'I suppose so. Sixteen million dollars, you said?'

'Plus whatever the General costs this time.'

Pipe sat in silence for a while, stabbing at his blotter with a paperknife. 'I don't know what you'll have to do, George,' he said slowly, 'but sixteen million dollars is, by the grace of God, a lot of sterling. Furthermore, if the dockers and railwaymen oblige with a nice stoppage or the Chancellor says something stupid, which he will do, given the chance, sterling may do us a favour and weaken a bit, which would be very nice and would make the whole thing sit well on the page in the Annual Report. To lose that much to the bloody French, of all people, would be yet another nail in our beloved country's coffin.'

'And in ours.'

'And, as you say, in ours. You have my authority to buy the business, and if you ever say as much I shall deny it.'

'I didn't need it. I was going to buy it anyway.'

'Just don't tell me what you have to do, that's all. So that if it ever comes into court I don't have to commit perjury. Or not a great deal of perjury.'

'You're ever the leader, Rufus, out in front of your platoon there, waving your little baton as you lead them into the murderous enemy fire. Taking the responsibility, what?'

'Shut up,' Pipe said. 'You know perfectly well the Chairman and I have to be protected in such matters.'

On his way out of Pipe's office, George Pidduck stopped at Daphne's desk. 'About tonight,' he said.

'Yes, my hair'll be dry by nine. Come round then, my sweet.' She had finished her bun and coffee and had retouched her lipstick.

'Fact is, Daph, I have to catch a plane to Jakarta.'

'Damn,' Daphne said, pouting her generous, perfectly outlined mouth and creasing her beautiful forehead in a frown. 'I really fancied you tonight, George.'

'Me too, Daph, me too. But duty calls. I'll bring you a bit of batik or something from Jakarta.'

She smiled, looking him in the eyes. She knew how inordinately beautiful she was. 'Never mind, my sweet. I'll keep it all warm for you.'

George Pidduck leant over and kissed her cheek. 'Maybe I'll stop off in Rome on the return flight and you'll join me there. We can fly back together the next day.'

'I'd like that, my sweet.'

'Great. Oh, and try not to call me "my sweet" in the office.'

After he'd gone, Daphne put her head round Pipe's door. 'If you can hold your lust in check till nine,' she said, 'you could come round then. I think my hair will be dry.'

9

'Wonderful,' Rufus Pipe said. 'You've made me very happy, Daphne.'

And he blew her a kiss.

These events explain the presence of George Pidduck, Sales Director of All World, at the Shangri-La in Singapore.

CHAPTER
2
―――――――――

'So tell me what the hell is going on,' George Pidduck
said. The three of them were by the pool of the Shangri-
La. It was just after nine in the morning. He had slept
well and felt as good as he ever did on the morning after
a long flight. In the pool two Chinese children splashed
rather solemnly under the eye of a Malay nurse.

'It is confusion,' Mr Sombolon replied. 'It is damn bad
confusion. I am informed first that our contract is safe.
Then I am informed that the General is seeing
difficulties. I hear stories of the Japanese and the
Americans and then the damn French. This surprises
me, for who are the damn French in the oil business? I
use my excellent influences. I see the General. He talks
to me of fish.'

'Fish?'

'Yes, Mr Pidduck, of fish. You see, fish indicates
fishing. For good fishing in Indonesian waters you need
a boat. That is sensible. It is the General's wish to go
fishing.'

'So he was hinting that he wants a boat. So what's
wrong with that?'

'Nothing is at all wrong. Indeed, I presumed on your
behalf to offer him all our facilities for a very fine boat.
I sought advice from Mr Macarthur here and I was
informed that very fine boats are made in the Davani
yard at Genoa, isn't it? So I offer the General a Davani
power boat. I am informed that it costs 500 million lire.
That is Italian money. No doubt we can negotiate a
better price.'

'So what happened?'

'The General acts damn strange. He says okay. Then
he says no longer okay. I ask what I can do that is better

than a Davani boat. He will not say. He sends me away. I seek another meeting. He will not grant it. So I use my important connections and I learn that the General will award the contract to the damn French. I am mystified, Mr Pidduck. I lose face. I am humiliated before you.'

'Never mind that, Mr Sombolon,' George Pidduck said. 'What I want to know is what the French offered him to make him change his mind. After all, he knows that with us all he needs to do is name it and he can have it.'

'Very beautifully expressed, Sir,' Mr Sombolon said. 'It is a very fine thought. Unfortunately, my excellent connections have not so far permitted me to discover what the French have offered.'

'Who represents them in Jakarta?'

'They have no one there. A man came from Paris – a small Frenchman, as small as me – and went to see the General. With him was another Frenchman from their embassy. I have the names. One damn visit and the General would no longer deal with his good friend Sombolon. I lose face.' He shook his head sadly.

'What do you make of it Sandy?' Pidduck asked Macarthur.

'I don't know. Maybe what the fellow really wants is an ocean-going yacht. Say 500 tons or so. I know of one on offer here in the Pi Ying yard.'

Mr Sombolon shook his head. 'If General Nasturtion wants 500 tons, Sir, he would ask his old friend Sombolon for 500 tons. He is a man who declares what he wants.'

'That's right,' Pidduck said. 'A fellow who can ask you for half a million dollars and a Corniche with gilt fittings all in one breath is a man who declares what he wants.'

'So what are you going to do?'

'I am going to find out what the French have offered and I'm going to do better,' Pidduck said.

'I have been thinking greatly,' Mr Sombolon said. 'Respectfully, my thinking goes this way. Our great

12

company has won contract for past seven years against many competitions and many beastly offers to the General. Always when the Japanese offer him a million he acts with great honour and kindness towards us. He says: "Japanese offer is one million. For one and quarter you have the business." And he never organizes auction. So always we have much appreciation of our position, isn't it.'

'Quite.'

'But now what is happening? These Frenchmen make an offer and the General does not say: "Sombolon, my friend, I have been offered so and such by these Frenchmen. What can your great company do?" No, he refuses to see me. That is strange.'

'Very.'

'So I think: what can Frenchmen offer so specially that it cannot be beaten by our great company?'

'And what's your answer?'

Mr Sombolon shook his head. 'I do not know. I think perhaps in your great wisdom and infinite informations of the world, you will know what is special for the Frenchman to offer.'

'Birds,' George Pidduck said.

'Birds?'

'Birds. Women. They specialize in women. Maybe he's heard about it.'

'That is not possible. My own informations in this thing are very good. The General has – how do you say it – the hots for fat German ladies. Only lately he asked me as a special favouring to find him three more.'

'Really?'

'Yes. Fifty inches in the bottoms.'

'Christ!' Pidduck said. 'Did you do it?'

'Of course. I have damn extraordinary connections.'

'Quite. So it probably isn't French birds. What else?'

'The French are famous for their food,' Sandy said, 'but he can't be taking it all in foie gras and chocolate eclairs.'

There was a gloomy silence. 'There is *nothing* the

13

French can do that we can't do better,' George Pidduck said at last. 'I may be stumped now, but I don't intend to stay in that condition. We will go to Jakarta and we will turn the bloody place upside down until we find out what that little bugger's been offered and what we have to do to cap it. Tell me, Mr Sombolon, how long have we got before they have to exchange letters of intent?'

'The law requires opening of bids tomorrow and formal allocation of contracts two days later. Then letters of intent one week after. I can make it twenty days, Sir.'

'How do you do that?'

'My very good friend in the Ministry of Mines is in charge of contracts. He is a big man. I will telephone him today and he will lose the bids for some days. It is not expensive. Maybe five hundred dollars US in his account at the Hong Kong & Shanghai Bank here in Singapore.'

'Fix that,' Pidduck instructed. 'Sandy, you look after the details.'

'Sure.'

'That will give us three weeks in all. Should be enough.'

'You have great wisdom and business principles,' Mr Sombolon said happily. 'I said to my damn wife: "Mr George Pidduck will come from London. He is a very big man there and he will find all answers that Sombolon is too foolish and ignorant to find." And my wife says: "That is a very true statement." She is a foolish woman but she is the mother of my children and I think I am the father.'

'Quite.'

'They are also probably foolish,' Mr Sombolon added.

'Nonsense,' Pidduck said, getting up. 'Now let's go and see your friend at the embassy.'

The taxi took them down Orchard Road, past the great hotels, to the large and handsome Indonesian Embassy. Its sophisticated blend of Eastern and Western architectural influences was misleading. Inside the visa section, the East had taken over in its leisurely and amiable fashion. There was a queue made up of people whose expressions and posture bespoke resignation before the inevitability of delay, procrastination and confusion. The clerks were numerous behind the counters. They were doing a good deal of writing on forms and in books. Names were called from time to time. Passports were handed in and, on occasion, out.

'All this is damn nonsense,' Mr Sombolon said. 'Please kindly wait. I will see my very good friend Mr Dipa Supit. He is also my cousin. He is very big man in temporary visa subsection of visa section of our embassy. He will give you a very fine visa. Meanwhile, you will most kindly fill out the form.' He went to the counter and waved to a lean and wizened compatriot, who failed to see him. Then he shouted and the man looked up, caught sight of Mr Sombolon and smiled. He came over and they embraced warmly. There followed five minutes of animated conversation. Mr Sombolon turned to George Pidduck.

'My friend Mr Dipa Supit here has very great influence, as I told you. He can get you visa in one half normal time. You will leave your passport with him and he will keep it very carefully.'

'When will I have my visa?'

'Tomorrow at five. That is fantastic speed for visa and he will request only twenty-five dollar US.'

'But that's useless. I need it now. I want to be on a flight this afternoon.'

There was more animated talk. 'Mr Dipa Supit says it cannot be done. Normally visa takes two days. For respect and admiration of you, he will do one day, twenty-five dollars only. I am telling him you are a damn big man in England, isn't it?' Mr Sombolon had collected his English piecemeal over the years from the Americans, a Dutchman or two and a close friend who was a moneylender from Madras.

'No good,' George Pidduck said. 'Tell him if he does that to me, I lose face with my company. Ask him how

15

much for a visa now.'

They talked again. This time there were expressive gestures and a certain amount of shrugging of shoulders. 'Mr Dipa Supit is a reasonable man,' Sombolon said. 'He asks not a hundred dollars, not seventy-five dollars, not sixty dollars. He asks only fifty dollars.'

'Singapore dollars?'

'US dollars.'

'Okay.'

Mr Dipa Supit smiled broadly and took the passport and completed form back to his desk. A few minutes later he returned. The visa appeared to be in order.

'I have already yesterday paid him the fifty dollars commission on your behalf,' Sombolon said. 'I knew this would be your decision.'

They all shook hands amid smiles. On the way out a notice caught George Pidduck's eye. It said that temporary visas for tourism and business would be granted in twenty-four hours and that in exceptional circumstances requests for immediate visas would be favourably considered. It was all good training, he reflected, for dealing with General Nasturtion, Chairman of Entakan, the Indonesian national oil, tin mining and steel giant – the largest corporation in Asia.

They flew the sixty minutes to Jakarta that afternoon by Garuda. George Pidduck knew he had no hope of winning the argument about airlines with Mr Sombolon. This was because Mr Sombolon had a distant relative in the Garuda booking office in Singapore through whom he would buy the tickets at a discount, have them priced at the full fare and subsequently obtain his discount by means of a credit note made out to S.S. Sombolon. This credit note he would turn into cash via another friend in the Garuda accounts department, and the sum thus realized would be shared with his relative in the booking department. None of this would he have denied if challenged. It was a modest reward for a useful service rendered. Even the fiction that there were no seats on other airlines failed to trouble his conscience. He had said this information came from Garuda, and so it did. 'Tell the Englishman there are no seats on KLM, Cathay Pacific or Singapore Airlines,' his relative had said, and he had told him.

The monsoon had been drenching down onto the Indonesian islands for several weeks and nothing would stop it now for another couple of months. Water was pouring out of the heavens as their aircraft broke through the low cloud ceiling and eased down onto the runway at Jakarta airport. There had already been three inches of rain since dawn and the readings were heading steadily for another inch before sunset. The great thundering sheet of water poured out of the leaden sky and splashed noisily into the miniature lakes and torrents it was creating everywhere. As the water came down, the steaming vapour rose and saturated the atmosphere, so that shelter from the rain seemed to be little better than exposure to it. When the aircraft doors were open they each took their umbrella from the bedraggled member of the ground staff who had trundled them out to the plane. George Pidduck splashed his way across the hundred yards of open space to the terminal building, the rain driving at him under the umbrella, the puddles flooding his shoes. 'Why the hell does this have to happen plumb in the middle of the monsoon?' he muttered miserably to himself. 'Sod the little bastard for getting me into this.' He had no way of knowing that he was still, so to speak, in the shallow end. By the time he and Mr Sombolon were installed in a taxi and heading for the city, he was sodden and wrapped in despondency. When he moved his toes he could feel water.

Later they sat, shivering in the fierce air-conditioning, in enormous wicker armchairs in the bar of the Hotel Surabaya, peering at each other through the funereal gloom which the hotel's American design consultants had specified as *de rigueur* for bars. Pidduck felt his way to his double gin and tonic and took a long, helpful draught. Mr Sombolon toyed with a tumbler packed with crushed ice into the interstices of which a couple of fluid ounces of a locally produced cola drink had been poured. He had asked for a Coca-Cola.

'What do you suggest?' George Pidduck asked.

'Tonight,' Mr Sombolon replied, 'I see my many good friends. I discover where is the General. I get informations on the Frenchmen where they are. Tomorrow morning I report to you and make humble suggestions.'

'Good. Why don't you go off and start all that now? I'll have a meal here and an early night. My head's still in London.'

'Can I not take you to Ancol?' Mr Sombolon asked. 'Maybe to meet nice Indonesian lady?'

'Not tonight, Mr Sombolon. Tonight I must sleep.'

'Very good, Sir. Perhaps another night. In Ancol I know beautiful girl who comes from Aceh where they have very fine women. She is crazy for Englishmen.'

'We'll see about that,' George Pidduck said, getting up and groping his way past stools and low tables to reach the light. They bade each other goodnight and Mr Sombolon made his way out into the downpour and hailed a taxi to take him beyond Pasar Ikat to the old quarter with its ramshackle houses strung along the canals – now rushing torrents of muddy water. Here he had more family and many friends. Here also he had his own home in a large stuccoed house which hovered uneasily in style between Dutch colonial and ethnic Javanese. But he headed instead for the house of his brother, Pak Sombolon MD, which was nearby. Once the home of a solid Dutch trader, it was now the most substantial residence in the district, and though Dr Sombolon's wife had been urging him for years to move the family out to the middle-class comforts of Menteng, he refused to budge. This was because of a law requiring all transfers of property within the city to be approved by the Governor. Dr Sombolon had no objection to this law, nor even to its consequence: that the Governor would require a contribution to his personal funds in return for appending

18

the essential initials to the instrument of transfer. What he did object to was the fact that the General, who had been Governor of Jakarta for the past five years, was inordinately greedy, even as Generals went. He was pricing his initials at such an extortionate level that virtual paralysis had seized the property market. Furthermore, the man designated to succeed him was a patient and a bridge partner of the Doctor's and would certainly cost, between old friends, far less. So he waited to move out to Menteng and meanwhile was devoting most of his substantial income to buying gold and smuggling it, ounce by ounce, to Singapore.

His brother was not unconnected with this tricky pursuit and there was an arrangement between them which resulted for Mr Sombolon in a useful commission calculated on the official gold price on the Singapore market at the time of arrival of each consignment. These commissions Mr Sombolon paid into the Singapore branch of the Algemeine Bank Nederland for transfer to an account of his in Amsterdam. He maintained bank accounts in five countries, reckoning that the combination of economic disaster and Red revolution that haunted him whenever his thoughts turned to the future, was unlikely to hit all five of the countries he had chosen at the same time. They were Singapore itself, Holland, Switzerland, the USA (about whose fiscal policies he was beginning to harbour grave doubts) and Kuwait. Though he was the agent for All World, a British company, he had no high opinion of the UK economy and kept no money in London. But if he could have hedged his bets with banks in Moscow and Peking he would certainly have done so. Tirana also appealed to him: he liked the combative neutrality of the Albanians.

Greetings and pleasantries once exchanged with his brother and his brother's wife and daughters, the females of the household withdrew and the brothers confronted each other with smiles and a certain amount of jovial banter.

'Tell me,' his brother said. 'What is your progress with these Western corrupters?'

'This time it is all very difficult,' Mr Sombolon replied. 'I have fears for my own arrangements with the English company. If I cannot win this contract I will earn no commissions next year. Also, they may be angry and seek another agent.'

They sipped strong coffee. Mr Sombolon lit a thin black cigar and stretched himself among the cushions on the low divan.

'What do you plan to do?' his brother asked.

'I must reach General Nasturtion through one of the German whores. For this I need your help. If we succeed I will bring fine gifts for your women.'

'Never mind that,' his brother said. 'We are brothers and we help each other. What do you want me to do?'

'You understand I cannot easily talk to the German women. He has them watched all the time, as you know very well. But as their doctor you can visit them without arousing suspicion. Is any of them sick at present?'

'The Glauber girl has a female complaint. I am treating her with an ointment from America. The General got it for me through the embassy in Washington.' He smiled at the thought of such a product coming from such a source. Then his mind returned to Glauber. 'Such succulent thighs,' he said. 'And the pubis is blonde!' He shook his head sadly.

Mr Sombolon told his brother exactly what he wanted him to arrange with Hildegarde Glauber the next day. Then he spent nearly an hour at the telephone and finally made his way home.

CHAPTER
3

Next morning in George Pidduck's suite Mr Sombolon reported progress. 'The General is visiting the Entakan refinery at Riau. That is in Sumatra,' he said. 'His return is not known. Also, the small French man is here in Jakarta. Room 606 in this hotel. Very fortunate. His name is . . .' he consulted a small piece of paper '. . . Bernard de Brives de Moustier. A strange name. Also I hope to get informations on General's desires and offerings of damn Moustier.'

'How will you get that?' Pidduck asked.

'For money one of the German girls will do it most certainly.'

'How much money?'

'Not big. Maybe ten thousand dollars US.'

'Christ, that's bloody outrageous!'

'With respects, it is reasonable for good informations leading to contract.'

'I won't pay that kind of money.'

'Then there may be cheaper way.' A slow and mysterious smile spread over Mr Sombolon's subtle brown features. He looked down as he spoke: no loss of face must be caused in the event that what he had to say offended this gross Westerner, normally so insensitive to shades of meaning and the true nature of self-respect. 'This German woman,' he said slowly, picking his way through the words on some kind of tiptoe, 'for many months now she only makes love with the General.' He paused, and added: 'Not very often, according to my informations, and not with best satisfactions. She shares with four other German ladies and maybe others.'

'How do you know?' Pidduck asked, intrigued despite

21

his mistrust of Mr Sombolon's complex mental processes, and unaware as yet of the direction the dialogue was about to take.

'My brother, Pak Sombolon MD, is doctor to German ladies,' Mr Sombolon said with a touch of family pride. 'Also, I have some good informations from servants at house where German women are living under General's careful protection.'

'I see. Go on.'

'So my thinkings are respectfully as following.' He continued to look at the floor. 'She is very fine woman. Very white. Very soft. She likes to make love. And yet – how do you say it so delicately – she is not getting enough. This is according to my best understandings. And so I believe much appreciations would be caused to her if you. . .' his fingers traced expressive shapes in the air '. . . if you gave her your excellent lovings.' He paused, and mistaking George Pidduck's stupefied silence for careful and judicious examination of his proposal, he added: 'Very discreetly arranged, you understand. With no danger for the General to know.'

George Pidduck found his voice. 'Let me be sure I've got it right. You're telling me you want me to have it off with one of General Nasturtion's German tarts in order to get information, and that will cost me less than the ten thousand dollars.'

'Your understandings,' Mr Sombolon said happily, looking up for the first time, 'are perfection.'

'I'd sooner pay the money,' Pidduck said.

'Very good, if you prefer. I do personally think this is best way.'

'But ten *thousand* . . . it's bloody steep!'

'Other way, only five thousand. I can arrange.'

'Other way, she should pay *me*,' Pidduck said. 'What does she look like?'

Mr Sombolon was equal to the occasion. From his pocket he took a well-thumbed envelope and passed it over without a word. He was smirking, and allowed himself an almost inaudible chuckle. George Pidduck extracted from the envelope half a dozen colour snapshots. They had been taken by flash in a heavily over-decorated bedroom. Each of them showed a grouping of five plump girls. They were striking a series of heroic poses, in which they were assisted by their equipment. Each held a long spear and wore a helmet of vaguely Norse aspect, and each had on a cloak fastened at the neck. All the cloaks were flung back behind them, revealing the fact that all were stark naked. On each photograph they were posed differently though always heroically. They all looked stolidly into the camera, devoid of all expression. It was the least erotic set of dirty postcards he'd ever seen.

'One on left is Hildegarde,' Mr Sombolon said. 'Very soft.'

'Hildegarde?'

'Yes, Hildegarde Glauber. Forty-eight inches when she arrives. Now fifty-one. She eats plenty saté and also cookies.' Mr Sombolon seemed to think this was a bull point.

Pidduck groaned. 'Why the fancy dress, Mr Sombolon, tell me that.'

'The General paid visit to New York to lead delegation selling crude. So oil company invites him to opera. He sees German opera – much singing and shouting. "Terrible noise," he tells me later. "Our gamelan orchestras much better." But on stage he sees women dressed like this, but with robes on, you understand. Lady warriors, I believe. I do not know such operas. But for him that is very sexy. And so he requested us for German girls last year, isn't it.'

'I see,' Pidduck said miserably. He shuddered. 'I can't do it,' he said. 'I'll do most things for the company, God knows, but I can't screw a bloody Valkyrie with a fifty-one-inch arse and a bloody helmet on her head.'

'Helmet can be removed,' Mr Sombolon said helpfully.

Pidduck shook his head. '*And* five thousand dollars,' he mumbled. 'That *and* five thousand.' He looked more closely at the pictures. 'Face isn't bad,' he said, 'but I never did find plump women were a turn-on, and this one's plump all right.'

'Very fine woman,' Mr Sombolon said. 'Very soft and white. Very sexy.' He was warming to his sales pitch.

'Shut up,' Pidduck said. 'You sound like a pimp at an auction.'

'Much regrets,' Mr Sombolon said, recovering his dignity. 'Please keep pictures with my compliments.'

'I tell you what. You go and find this Hildegarde Glob, or whatever she calls herself, and you tell her she can have two thousand if she delivers the goods, and that's that. But no naughty games thrown in.'

'I will try,' Mr Sombolon said, 'but I fear no successes.' He said this because his plan was for George Pidduck to pay not a penny less than five thousand, and the full ten if he could get it. All World Oil Services, having made a profit to his certain knowledge of thirty-six million dollars last year, could certainly afford ten thousand to be shared between himself, his brother and the Glauber woman. All he had to do now was to make sure she played ball. And she certainly would.

'Today,' he said, 'I must do many things and see many persons. I will speak with Hildegarde Glauber also. I will report to you at eight o'clock, isn't it.'

'Good,' George Pidduck said. 'I'll amuse myself till then. I've got plenty of mail to catch up on. Be here at eight, then, and we'll eat some saté somewhere.'

'And maybe you like to meet lady from Aceh?' Mr Sombolon had a simple view of Western tastes.

'We'll see,' Pidduck said.

It was still raining when he went down for a drink before lunch. He plunged into the obscurity of the bar and after barking a shin on the sharp corner of a table, ended up perched on a stool, peering across the bar in search of the barman. Seeing him suddenly only a few inches away, he ordered a gin and tonic. On the next seat he could make out the small figure of a man. When

24

this troglodyte ordered a drink he detected the French accent. He could be getting lucky.

'Terrible rain,' he said.

'Certainly terrible.'

'You been here long?'

'This time one week. And you?'

'Only a day, but I may have to stay wet for a couple of weeks.'

'Ah.'

'You here on business?'

'Yes.'

'So am I. Are you in oil?'

'I am in a closely related field.'

'With the Compagnie Française des Pétroles?'

'No.'

For a Frenchman, he was cagey. Indeed, for almost anyone he was cagey. But by now, his size combined with his reticence and his grudging admission that he was more or less in oil, had convinced Pidduck that he was talking to de Brives de Moustier. Minor aristocrat, Pidduck decided. Or more likely the 'de's' were fakes. The French were always doing that. Refusing to accept the French Revolution. He called the barman through the gloom and tried again.

'Give me another double gin,' he said, 'and this gentleman will have . . .' he turned to the diminutive Frenchman, perched like a baby owl in the dark '. . . What are you drinking?'

'Thank you, a scotch and soda.'

The drinks arrived. 'Cheers,' Pidduck said. 'Here's to a successful trip.'

'Thank you, and for you also.'

'Difficult, doing business with the Indonesians.'

'Very.'

'Always have to find the one man who can say yes or no.'

'Absolutely.'

'And look after him.'

'Certainly.'

'I'm selling tugboats,' Pidduck lied. 'Trying to negotiate a contract for six vessels with Entakan, but I can't
seem to reach the man who counts.'

'In Entakan there is only one man,' the Frenchman
said, unable to resist parading a little superior knowledge.

'I deal with their head of procurement.'

'Useless, my friend. *Sans intérêt.*'

'Really?'

'As I say, there is only one man to decide in Entakan.'

'Who is that?'

'General Nasturtion.'

'The Chairman?' Pidduck didn't mind sounding like
an ignorant fool if it was going to lead somewhere.

'Yes. He controls personally all expenditures above
100,000 dollars.'

'And takes a . . . commission?' Pidduck saw the owl's
head nod in the shadows. 'Do you know the General?'
he asked.

'I do.'

'Have you been – successful with him?'

'I have. I am here to settle the formalities.'

'Well done!' Pidduck said with as much bonhomie as
he could muster. 'Jolly good! *Très bien!*'

'Thank you.'

There was a silence. It was hard going. 'I must take
your advice and ask to see the General,' Pidduck said.
'Is he in Jakarta?'

'At present he is travelling but he should be back by
the end of the week. That is when I have to see him
myself.'

'Competition fierce in the oil business?'

'Very fierce. *Epouvantable.*'

Silence again. A plan of sorts was forming in
Pidduck's mind. Problem is how to loosen this tiny
Frenchman's tongue. Solution 1: get him drunk. Solution 2: *cherchez la femme.* Pidduck thought he might be
on to something there. He would need Mr Sombolon's
help. It was maddening how he always found himself

26

needing the help of that dubious ally. But if it worked it would be far cheaper than the ridiculous German plan.

'Care to join me for a meal this evening?' he asked. 'I know a first-class place for Javanese food over towards Fatahilah Square. Absolutely no tourists. An Indonesian friend takes me there.'

'That is very kind,' the Frenchman said. 'The food here at the hotel is fairly disgusting. I shall be delighted to try your restaurant. Permit me to introduce myself: Bernard de Brives de Moustier.'

'George Pidduck.'

They shook hands. 'Let's meet in the lobby at eight,' Pidduck said.

He killed the rest of the day by working his way doggedly through his briefcase. At seven he called Rufus Pipe at home and woke him out of a deep sleep to tell him it wasn't going to be easy. 'Gladys is working on a plan but Muriel is away till the end of the week,' he said.

'Who the hell are Gladys and Muriel?' Pipe asked. He had forgotten Pidduck's explanation of the cover names in the cable and in any case, he was still half asleep.

'You know, Rufus . . . Gladys and Muriel. I explained to you.'

'Can't remember you explaining anything about two birds called Gladys and Muriel. Why don't you get on with the Entakan job instead of chasing after the other?'

'They aren't birds.'

'So what the hell are they, transvestites?'

'Oh, forget it. Never mind. I'll call you again when I have anything worth reporting.'

Later, when he presented himself once more in the hotel lobby, Mr Sombolon was exuding confidence. He had had a busy day, sustained and fortified by the aroma of gain growing with delightful pungency in his nostrils as he beavered away at his plans. If, despite everything, All World failed to win the contract this time, he would at least have earned himself a few thousand out of the peripheral activities. It accorded with his deeply held conviction that nothing should ever be done for nothing. Payment by results, he reasoned, was a very fine principle indeed. But allied to a supplementary system of payment according to effort expended, it was the very distillation of human justice. These were the guidelines he was following. 'It is very good,' he told Pidduck. 'The Glauber girl is willing for getting informations from the General.'

'For two thousand?'

'For ten thousand.'

'Nothing doing.'

Mr Sombolon shrugged. He had expected to fail at ten thousand. He turned to his fall-back plan. 'Please, I told her about you. I said you are fine Englishman, very interested in ladies and always giving great satisfactions in loving.'

'You said that?'

'Yes, Sir.'

'And how the hell do you know whether I give satisfactions, as you put it, or not?'

'Last year I am told by that girl in Surabaya. You remember, perhaps, at the Hotel Indonesia. She tells me: "Oh, that Englishman, he . . ."'

'All right, never mind,' Pidduck said. He was pleasantly flattered and would have liked to hear the rest of the sentence but felt it hardly appropriate. 'So what happened?'

'Hildegarde Glauber is happy to follow second plan.'

'Which means?'

'Smaller payment. Also sex.'

'How much?'

Mr Sombolon's eyes sought the floor. These Westerners were crude beyond belief. 'I do not know how much sex you can offer and so I did not fix with her. It is perhaps matter for negotiation between you.'

'Not how much sex, Mr Sombolon. How much cash.'

'Six thousand dollars.'

'Ridiculous. Forget it.'

'I may persuade for five.'

'Far too much. And in any case, I have a better plan which may cost us nothing at all.'

Mr Sombolon did not like the sound of what he heard. 'Please?'

'I've met the Frenchman.'

'Yes?'

'And he's dining with us tonight. He thinks I'm here trying to sell tugs to Entakan.'

Mr Sombolon nodded and said nothing.

'My plan,' Pidduck said, 'is to get him drunk and see if he'll talk. Failing that, what about your lady friend out at Ancol? Maybe she could get something out of him if you brief her carefully.'

'A very fine scheme,' Mr Sombolon said without conviction. His agile mind was climbing over and under this perfectly reasonable proposal, seeking chinks through which it could be penetrated and destroyed. But for the moment the Englishman must be flattered. 'It is truly brilliant idea,' he said, winding himself up a little. 'A production of great experience in dealing with damn competition. I permit myself to congratulate you.'

'Thanks,' Pidduck said. He was inclined to agree with this assessment. 'Here he is, anyway.' Bernard de Brives de Moustier was approaching with small, springy steps across the lobby. Seen in the full light he was more like a chaffinch than a baby owl. He was small, neat, precise, trimly moustached and topped out with bristling ginger hair standing straight up from his scalp to a length of an inch or so, at which point an aggressive barber had chopped it short. His movements were darting and birdlike and his eyes, behind rimless glasses, were small and reasonably cunning. He was inappropriately dressed in a dark lounge suit of impeccable cut and he wore a tie. Mr Sombolon judged him to be a hopeless subject for a plan of the type devised by the Englishman.

Introductions were made and they shook hands. 'Mr Sombolon here will take us to this terrific restaurant,' Pidduck said. 'Let's have a drink in the bar before we go.'

They went to the bar. Mr de Brives de Moustier drank scotch-and-sodas. Pressed, he had four and then insisted enough was enough. He was steadier on his feet than George Pidduck as they felt their way around the furniture to get out into the light.

'Hey, I just thought of something,' Pidduck whispered to Mr Sombolon as they waited for their taxi. 'Does this place of yours serve liquor?'

'Certainly,' Mr Sombolon said.

The meal was good. Mr de Brives de Moustier drank steadily throughout and showed scarcely a trace of intoxication. Birdlike, he twittered with satisfaction over the beef rendang, which was exceedingly hot on the palate but seemed not to bother him at all. 'Excellent,' he kept saying, helping himself and washing the food down with draughts of scotch and soda. 'Truly excellent.' But beyond this he could be induced to say very little, and whenever Pidduck introduced the subject of Entakan, he would smile mysteriously and return to the subject of the food.

'What about a trip out to Ancol?' Pidduck suggested, making his last throw as the chendol followed the beef and coffee was served. 'Mr Sombolon here can fix it. He knows a very nice girl from Aceh, don't you, Mr Sombolon?'

Mr Sombolon smiled. It was a genuine smile because the danger was passing. This tiny Frenchman could clearly drink the Englishman under the table. He became less talkative, it seemed, the more alcohol he consumed. Mr Sombolon, as a good Moslem of the old school, regarded intoxication by means of alcohol as one of the more disgusting and inexplicable Western habits and could never understand why grown men and women were so intent on reducing themselves to the level of babbling idiots. This Frenchman, at least, preserved his dignity. As for the girl in Ancol, she would present no problem at all. If the Frenchman wanted her and she was willing, he would tell Pidduck that he had briefed her to dig for information. He would, of course, do no such thing.

'Certainly,' he said, 'we will find young lady at casino in Ancol. She is good friend of mine and she tells me many times she is very hot for French gentlemen.'

In the vast gambling room of the casino they played modest roulette and Mr Sombolon disappeared for a while. By the time their stock of chips had been taken from them and Mr de Brives de Moustier had firmly refused another drink at the bar, Mr Sombolon was seen ushering towards them two Indonesian girls of an undoubted beauty which they had done their best to spoil with heavy make-up. Introductions were made and the five of them trooped off awkwardly to the bar, where the girls ordered a fruit concoction and giggled encouragingly whenever Pidduck or the Frenchman opened their mouths. This ritual continued for twenty minutes with Mr Sombolon hovering on the sidelines like the pimp that, on this occasion, he was. He then exchanged a few words with the girls in their own language and announced that they would follow them back to the hotel in an hour and the price would be fifty dollars each.

'Just for a drink,' the Frenchman said.

'Yes, just for a drink,' Pidduck echoed.

Mr Sombolon could not understand why men insensitive enough to weaken their faculties publicly by the use of alcohol should be so reticent and apparently shy over such a straightforward and normal function as obtaining sexual satisfaction. Once he had asked his brother about it, since doctors could be expected to know something of these matters.

'A doctor called Freud explained it all,' Dr Sombolon had said. 'It is because in the West their mothers do not give the breast enough. It makes the men uncomfortable with women.'

'Why?'

'I do not know why. You would have to ask Dr Freud. He also explains that it has something to do with their excretory functions. And in the West, according to this

Dr Freud, the men are afraid of having their members cut off.'

'As they cut off hands in Saudi Arabia?'

'No, no. It is only a fear. Governments in the West do not cut off members.'

'Extraordinary.'

'I think so too.'

Be all that as it may, the evening ended as Mr Sombolon planned it should end, and whatever passed between Bernard de Brives de Moustier and the girl from Aceh, it was not information about the Entakan contract. The way was thus left clear for the operation of Mr Sombolon's plan. This plan had been elaborated earlier that day in a series of encounters and negotiations of Eastern subtlety and deviousness, all centred around the person of the General's current favourite, Hildegarde Glauber.

'My brother, Mr S. S. Sombolon, would like to speak with you,' the doctor had said to her.

'*Warum*? Why that is?' Hildegarde asked.

'He has an interesting proposition to put before you. But there must be absolute discretion, you understand. The General would perhaps not be pleased.'

'*Jawohl*! That I understand.'

'I will take you to my surgery in my car,' the doctor said, 'and there you will talk with my brother. We will tell the people here you are coming for treatment for your intimate condition. I will see them.'

Hildegarde shrugged. She was not a girl who intervened much in her own life. She was inclined to do what she was asked to do, and when nothing was being asked of her she was inclined to do nothing at all. This porcine inactivity of spirit was admirably suited to her heavy but rather comely physique. She was a big girl – had always been a big girl – and she was built for durability and comfort rather than speed. Her mind was passive: it was also somewhat slow. Her movements were slow as well, nicely adjusted, it seemed, to the speed at which her mind could be induced to function. She was amiable, perhaps because she had neither the energy nor the initiative to be anything else. And she had come to Jakarta because someone had asked her nicely and she couldn't, in the time available, think of a reason not to come. That, and the useful sum in dollars that was proffered. She found money interesting, and because she held no strong views on anything – indeed, no views at all on most things – there was hardly anything she would not do for money, provided it did not have to be done in a hurry. In matters of money, indeed, Hildegarde Glauber had much of the persistence and cunning of her Swabian peasant forebears. As for the money itself, she hardly spent any of it. After all, what could money buy (apart from lipstick and romantic novels in paperback) that was better than money itself?

Untypically, Mr Sombolon came straight to the point. 'I have proposition,' he said. 'Very interesting for you. Much moneys.'

There was a flicker of interest in Hildegarde's pale blue eyes, but she said nothing because she could not think of anything to say.

'Yes,' Mr Sombolon continued, 'much moneys. Also much saucy fun.'

'*Ich verstehe nicht.* How is saucy fun?'

'Nice gentleman,' Mr Sombolon said.

Hildegarde showed no sign of interest. The proposal had a dreary ring of familiarity about it. 'Ladies I prefer,' she said. 'But gentleman is okay. Indonesian gentleman?'

'No, very fine English gentleman. Very big man in England. I believe he is brother to English Queen.' Mr Sombolon prided himself on his salesmanship.

'*Ach, ein Prinz!*' Hildergarde exclaimed.

'Perhaps not a Prince,' Mr Sombolon said, retreating a little from the edge of the hole he was digging for himself, 'but still a brother of the English Queen.'

'That cannot be,' Hildegarde said. Her mind might be slow, but once attached to a proposition it clung on for dear life. 'All brothers of Queen are *Prinzen*. Also

English Queen no brothers has. So I think.'

'Maybe a cousin, then,' Mr Sombolon said, 'but it has no importance. This English gentleman, he is very big man, very rich, and for you he is hot.'

This Hildegarde understood. And although she considered herself to be in love with Anneliese Schenk, she was not averse to a certain type of man and his money.

'*Also?*' she prompted.

'Englishman pay very big money for lovings and informations. Dollars US.'

'Informations? *Was ist das?*'

'Englishman makes big contract with Entakan. He must know what French company offers so he can make better offer to General Nasturtion.'

'This I know not,' Hildegarde said.

'But this you can ask General.'

Hildegarde considered Mr Sombolon's statement and slowly an understanding of the nature of his proposal began to germinate in her mind. She was to get information while in bed with the General and impart it while in bed with the Englishman and for this she would be paid. In US dollars.

'How many?' she asked, assuming that Mr Sombolon had been keeping somehow abreast of her thoughts.

'Please?'

'Dollars US. How many?'

'One thousand.'

This seemed to her like good money, but who ever accepted the first sum mentioned? She had learned this simple rule in her native village and had continued to live by it. '*Nein*', she said simply.

'Nine is too much,' Mr Sombolon said.

They sorted out the confusion. Then, after some argument, Hildegarde settled for fifteen hundred dollars. It was five hundred less than Mr Sombolon feared he would have to pay, and five hundred more than Hildegarde thought the whole thing was worth. Mr Sombolon then explained very slowly exactly what was expected of her. How she had to ask the General certain questions when she had him in the right frame of mind, and how she was expected to go to bed with the Englishman before getting the information from the General. This confused her a little but if it was what these people wanted, then it was what, in her amenable fashion, she would do for them. There was no way of telling from her expression whether she had really understood anything. She looked exactly as she had done in the photographs – absolutely blank. It worried Mr Sombolon, but at the end she said firmly: 'This I understand, *jawohl*!' And so his brother had returned her to the house and the waiting Anneliese Schenk, already perturbed by her long absence.

'I do not understand,' the doctor said later to his brother. 'This woman would do what is required for fifteen hundred dollars. Why do you then have to organize this difficult coupling with the Englishman?'

Mr Sombolon smiled. His brother was clever at medicine but he did not understand the ways of the world. At school Pak Sombolon had been busy staying at the top of the class while S.S., the younger of the two, had been even busier running a cold drink stand at the school gates, building in time to the control of cold drink concessions outside three other schools.

'It is simple,' he said, 'but to understand it you must also understand how these Westerners think. My calculation was that he can be persuaded to pay maybe five thousand dollars for this information. But if I ask for five thousand, what happens? He throws up his hands in horror. "Far too much! Ridiculous!" For Westerners believe always that in the East they will be robbed.'

'And will they not be?' the doctor asked gently.

'Certainly. But if we ask for ten when a service is worth five, it is because we have learned that our asking price will be greeted with hostility and derision.'

'A circular situation.'

'Possibly. I am no philosopher. But let us return to the Englishman and the German woman. If I calculated

35

that we could obtain five thousand, I had to start far higher. So I started at ten thousand. Now you may say, why not simply allow him to beat me down to the five that I want? The answer is simple: never do I want him to believe that the prices I quote to him for this or that can be driven down in such a manner. It would cause me a lot of trouble on future occasions. So I offer him a cheaper alternative: ten thousand without sex, five thousand with sex. This also has the advantage of being confusing, for usually something with sex would cost more than something without. So the Western mind, my dear brother, fastens itself onto this strange choice and no longer devotes proper attention to the price itself. And after a little fuss about the size of the sums, this is what the Englishman did.'

'Is he pleased about having this woman?'

'Not at all. But that does not matter. His alarm also helps him to forget how much he pays.'

'I see.'

'And I have a further calculation. I believe this woman is very passionate and I also have heard that the Englishman is a great performer with ladies. Put them together, and we may have a new situation with big possibilities. You will understand that where there is lust and passion there are often opportunities of all kinds. . .' He waved an expressive hand to denote the infinity of permutations that might issue from such a biological confrontation.

The doctor shook his head in admiration. 'You have great talent. You fully deserve your rewards.'

'Yes,' said his brother simply. 'I would not wish to receive money that I did not deserve.'

CHAPTER
4

Hildegarde Glauber's normally comatose personality
could be awakened by three things and three things
only: gold, carbohydrate and sex. Her appetite for all
three was prodigious, but now it was sex which fully
occupied her mind – fully because it was not a mind
capable of grappling with more than one proposition at
a time. So that now, in George Pidduck's suite, after a
generous but inarticulate dinner for two, she was naked
upon his bed – white-and-pink, blonde, blue-eyed
behind long, pale lashes, breathless and damp. She had
been finding this Englishman very much to her taste
and had settled down to enjoy herself.

She had learned long ago at her mother's knee that
God had made the earth and all things in it and upon
looking at His handiwork had permitted Himself a
feeling of satisfaction. So, if God had made all things,
He it was who had devised sex in all its fascinating
forms, and presumably He was as pleased with what He
had done in that area as He was with the butterflies and
flowers. Hildegarde had quite strong religious feelings
of a general kind and had always felt at ease with her
God in everything she did. For if He had made her and
all other creatures, including this Englishman, and had
equipped them in this fascinating way, how could He
object to the things they got up to? So she reasoned
slowly and carefully, building proposition on proposition in her mind like the more thoughtful type of
toddler with a set of educational bricks. And so she
concentrated now on enjoying her encounter with the
rugged and attractive Englishman.

Something of all this had naturally filtered across to
George Pidduck. Not that it was difficult to tell whether

Hildegarde was enjoying herself or not. For her orgasms, when her sluggish and unresponsive nervous system could be roused into action, were like the sudden eruptions of some long-dormant volcano – a great heaving and thrashing of huge white thighs and massive adipose tissue, accompanied by guttural cries of ecstasy which, heard unawares, were profoundly alarming. As her climax approached, she provided an impressive demonstration of the primal biological function, of Nature going about her business untrammelled by the limitations of cheaply constructed beds and the inadequacies of sound-insulation in a hotel built well below specification by a corrupt contractor. Her pectorals would have done credit to a Sydney lifeguard and she was using them to the full.

'*Ach!*' she cried. '*Gott in Himmel! Du bist Wunderschön – ach, mein Putzi!*'

'Don't call me Putzi, dammit. And try not to shout so much.'

Her flailing right foot caught him a nasty jab in the kidneys while the left one pounded his buttock, and he gasped with the sudden pain. She took it as a cry of passion. 'So again *mein Putzi* coming is,' she cooed into his ear in a rasping whisper. 'By me this *wunderbar und fantastisch* is. By *mein Putzi auch*, is not so?' And she tightened the vice-like grip of her knees about his battered torso and let out a deafening moan. Her nails dug deep into his trapezius.

'God,' he thought, 'what in the name of sanity am I doing here, locked into this steaming creature and receiving wounds left and right? Let's get it over with before she does me a serious injury.'

But this was no easy matter. They had been thrashing on the dangerously weakened bed for over two hours, and Pidduck, who had some cause to be proud of his sexual prowess, was nearing the end of his capacities with this insatiable woman. Not that the whole thing had been an irksome chore. Indeed, Pidduck was telling himself that he had had a very good time indeed. He was beginning to think he had missed out, all these years, on plump women. Enfolded in Hildegarde's plump but powerful arms and cushioned against her great Earth-mother breasts with their enormous pink nipples, strange emotions chased each other unbidden through his mind. He felt at once like a little boy in her embrace and an immensely virile male, proud that he was able to arouse so thoroughly such a very large female organism. It was, he thought, a bit like being at the wheel of a really powerful sports job. The merest touch on the pedal and you reached sixty in nine seconds. With this woman, a touch on the right spot produced a comparable displacement and outburst of energy and engine noise. Mr Sombolon, he reflected, must have been right: she hadn't been getting enough.

But in this he was profoundly mistaken: she had been in the arms of her beloved Anneliese every night for weeks past and had in fact arisen from Anneliese's bed to bathe and dress that afternoon, to be ready for Dr Sombolon to bring her to the hotel. There he had handed her on to his brother, who gave her her last-minute instructions.

'You will not talk to the Englishman about money.'

'*Jawohl.*'

'You understand, he is paying a lot. We have big expenses. Terrible expenses. We lose money on this.'

'*Jawohl,*' though she could not imagine what the expenses might be. But she knew all about the difference between what a client might pay and what a girl might end up with in her handbag.

'Also, you give him very good time.'

'*Natürlich.*' It had not occurred to her good-natured mind that she would do anything but her best for fifteen hundred dollars.

'You tell him you will surely get informations from General when he returns from Riau.'

'*Ja, ja.* I get.'

'Good,' Mr Sombolon said. Then he had another thought. 'Tell me, your trouble down there, all finished up?'

39

'All finished up,' she said. 'Now I am pure. Maybe I was pure before also and the *Herr Doktor* he likes to give ointments down there, no?'

Then Mr Sombolon had taken her to the bar and left her with Pidduck, promising to return for her at midnight. And this had led to food and then this *fantastisch* sex with this very competent Englishman who was a significantly better performer than the General, with no special interest in rubber, and boasting altogether more satisfactory dimensions.

Now, at last, George Pidduck lay bruised and exhausted on the bed. At his side, Hildegarde's metabolism was once again slowing down, her heartbeats returning to normal and her mind blanking out. Fed, satiated and soon to be financially rewarded, she wanted only to sleep. It had been a very satisfactory evening and she felt kindness and gratitude towards this obliging Englishman. '*Das war sehr Schön, mein Liebchen*,' she said in her rich and guttural Swabian accent, like low German filtered through faulty sound equipment.

Pidduck got the gist of it. 'Thanks,' he said. 'You were okay too. You were terrific.' Then he heard himself say: 'We must do this again.'

'*Jawohl*,' she replied with what was, for her, considerable animation.

'But first you have a little job to do for me.'

'*Ja, ja*, I do job. Then we make love plenty. We do new things together.'

Pidduck was too exhausted to ask what these new things might be. They both dozed until Mr Sombolon on the house phone announced that he was downstairs, waiting to take Hildegarde home.

General Nasturtion returned from Sumatra on the following day and that night he visited his German ladies. Warned of his arrival, they had carefully donned their equipment and greeted him with a tableau in which Anneliese lay naked upon a slab, like some kind of Aztec sacrifice, while the others brandished their spears above her most sensitive parts. There was a good deal of giggling by all save the sacrificial victim, who was afraid of being accidentally jabbed by one of her colleagues. Jealousy among the Germans was rampant. The General applauded between sips of champagne and called for more. Playfully (for women so sturdily built) they dragged him from his armchair. Hildegarde, dressed in helmet and centurion's boots and nothing more, went down on all fours, her truly awesome rump presented for the General's inspection. He was handed a crop by one of the others and pulled into position astride. The crop came down on the great white bottom and amid grunts from Hildegarde and squeals of idiot laughter from the others, he was trundled off round the room, a small brown tycoon atop a hefty German peasant.

The General, whose army career had been in the engineers and not in the cavalry, had an uncertain seat. Under the prodding and tickling of the other girls he soon collapsed on the Aubusson carpet with Hildegarde largely on top of him. The breath had been knocked out of his body but the blood was pumping satisfactorily into his member and getting pleasantly blocked there.

'Enough,' he cried. 'That was good. Now to more serious business.'

He pinched that part of Hildegarde's anatomy that was within closest reach, and after the brief pause required for the signal from nerve ending to brain to be translated by that sluggish organ into a response, she let out a guttural howl. The General did it again. This time, knowing he liked it, she clipped him so hard round the ear that his teeth were heard to rattle in his head. This seemed to please him greatly. 'Good, good!' he said as he retrieved his spectacles from the carpet. She dug him playfully in the ribs and he gasped for air. 'Wonderful!' he cried. Then he dismissed the rest of the girls, who retreated with a good deal of sulky muttering: to be chosen to retire with the General always meant gifts, sometimes in dollars.

41

He allowed Hildegarde to lead him into her room, where she prepared herself to minister to his unusual and rather repellent sexual tastes. As she busied herself with a large plastic sheet and other props, she went over carefully in her mind what it was that she had to find out . . . A French contract to service oil rigs; some special gift offered to the General; and that remarkable Englishman needed to know what it was so that he could offer something better and so win the contract.

Later, as the General lay contentedly smoking on her bed with everything mopped up and cleared away, Hildegarde got to work in her ponderous fashion. 'Well, *mein Nasty*,' she said, 'you have much business you are doing these days? Or do you time with your big Hilde spend?'

'I have a lot of business, as usual. But I will come to see you whenever I can.'

'Enough you do not come.'

'I will try to come more, but you know I have to travel a lot.'

'You travel much in coming days?'

'Yes, soon I must go to Europe on business.'

Hildegarde's mind recognized a possible opening. 'To *mein* country?' she asked.

'No, to France.'

This was proving easier than she had expected. '*Warum* France?' she asked.

'I will sign a big French contract next week,' the General said, 'and afterwards I must go to Paris.'

'You take big Hilde with you along, okay?'

'I cannot do that,' the General said. 'I have to go on official business. I will be seeing important officials. The newspapers will interview me and publish my picture.'

'Why *mein Nasty*'s picture in newspapers?'

'I will tell you a big secret,' the General said. 'Can you keep big secrets?'

'Also small.' She didn't like telling a lie, but her romantic nature had been stirred by the Englishman . . . that and fifteen hundred dollars.

'I will tell you,' the General said. He had been bursting to tell someone what was to happen in France. He had tried it on his wife but she had declared that, as usual, he was about to make a fool of himself. 'I am to receive from the President of the French Republic in person a very high decoration,' he said.

'*Mein Nasty* will be a Milord!' Hildegarde exclaimed. She was genuinely moved.

'No, no. I will receive the Legion of Honour. It is the highest French decoration. The French President himself has it. In my case, it is awarded for outstanding services to industry, technology, commerce and Indonesian-French understanding. Also to peace.'

Hildegarde wrestled with these concepts, trying to stack them in her mind for later retrieval. 'Why does the French President give you this?' she asked. 'Why suddenly so?'

'It has been arranged by a French friend in return for business favours. I have awarded his company this very important contract. Several million dollars. He has told the French President, who now wishes to meet me and give me his highest decoration.'

'*Wunderbar!*' Hildegarde said.

'But you must tell no one. There are jealous men who would say to the French President: "Don't do it. General Nasturtion is not a suitable man to receive this honour." And that way they hope to win the contract by offering me other rewards instead.'

'Which other men will do this thing to *mein Nasty*?'

'The Americans. Also the British and the Japanese.'

'The British perhaps can make you a Milord. Is not better?'

'They cannot do that. Only the Queen decides these things in England.'

Hildegarde considered this carefully. For if the Englishman was truly the Queen's brother, or even her cousin, surely he could fix it. One could certainly do these things among family. She was tempted to explain it to the General but remembered Mr Sombolon's strict instructions: listen, but do not talk. And so she rolled over onto the General, her mission accomplished, and though he could not breathe he did not protest.

Hildegarde proudly reported her success to Dr Sombolon when he visited her the following day. On these occasions he would give the girls extensive medical check-ups, having persuaded the General that this was standard practice in the West and would be regarded by the girls as a desirable perk. 'Also,' he pointed out, 'they will be clean, and that is important for you.'

'They are not going with other men,' the General replied, 'so how could they become diseased?'

'This can happen,' the doctor told him. 'There are cases of nasty venereal infection from the seats of these Western-style toilets.' It was a lie and he knew it.

'Very unhygienic, all those naked arses following each other on the same seat,' the General said. 'Our stand-up system is better.' He had agreed to the medical inspections and Dr Sombolon had built them up over the months into fortnightly groping and ogling sessions in which he palpated their rolling white breasts for – he said – dangerous lumps, and undertook unnecessarily detailed inspections and probing of their most intimate parts, prescribing creams for imaginary conditions of the vulva whenever he could, and applying them in person whenever the girls would let him. It had become his preferred way of spending a professional afternoon.

'Excellent,' the doctor said to Hildegarde. 'Tell me what you have learned.'

'*Nein*,' Hildegarde said. 'I wish to tell it to the *Englander* directly.'

'Why is that?'

'I love him, okay?'

'Yes, but you can tell me and my brother will tell the Englishman. Also, he will then pay you immediately.'

Lust and cupidity fought ponderously for possession of Hildegarde's mind and lust triumphed. 'I will to make love with the *Englander* again,' she said. 'Then I tell.'

Dr Sombolon reported this outcome to his brother. 'We must persuade the Englishman to do what is necessary,' he said. 'If he refuses, we may have trouble with the girl. She could even denounce us to the General, and that would be very bad for me.'

'Never fear,' his brother said. 'I will see that he accepts. But are you sure she has the information?'

'I cannot be sure but I think so. She is a simple girl.'

'Simple, maybe, but at present she has us dancing to her tune, not the other way round. So I hope you are right.'

Seeing George Pidduck at his hotel later, he broached the subject with some trepidation, fearing a typical outburst of undignified anger such as he had been taught was only to be expected from the ill-educated, the mentally unbalanced or from Westerners. 'I have much pleasures for you,' he said, accepting a cup of tea and declining an American muffin. 'I have informations looking excellently forward with much promising.' He was nervous and this was inclined to loosen what grip he had on English syntax.

'What is it, Mr Sombolon?' Pidduck asked.

'The German is reporting successes, yes. The General, I am told, has let dog out of basket.'

'Cat out of bag,' Pidduck said.

'Please?'

'The phrase is letting the cat out of the bag, but it doesn't matter. So what's the answer?'

'I do not know.'

'What do you mean?'

The whole thing was involving some loss of face for Mr Sombolon, who was acutely sensitive to the weakness of his position. He gazed resolutely into his teacup and refused to look up. 'So far I know certainly she has informations but so far she has not given them.'

'Why's that?'

Mr Sombolon took a deep breath. 'She says she will speak only to you.'

'Well, if that's all it is, arrange a meeting and she can tell me herself. Fix it for later today – whenever you like.'

'Not so easy, Sir,' Mr Sombolon said.

'Why not?'

'She will meet for informations only in – bedroom.'

To his surprise, the expected storm did not occur. He hazarded a glance from under his eyebrows at Pidduck, fearing that some seizure had prevented him from replying. But the man appeared to be perfectly calm. Even contented. 'I see,' he said finally. 'So I have to perform again, eh?'

Mr Sombolon gave an expressive shrug of his thin shoulders and said nothing. He still feared their interview was on a time fuse, with an explosion not far ahead. But no explosion came. He did not know that Pidduck had been thinking back on his encounter with Hildegarde, and the more he thought about it, the more appealing it seemed and the more his mind dwelt on the possibilities inherent in a reunion. Hadn't she talked of doing new things together? And was there not a lot of erotic mileage, as it were, to be got out of that great white body – at first so lethargic and then so tempestuous? Indeed there was. And the more he'd thought about it, the more clearly had he come to the conclusion that bruises and bite-marks notwithstanding, he would like to have Hildegarde Glauber again.

'Well, if I have to I suppose I must,' he said.

Mr Sombolon could hardly believe his ears. 'I am deeply sorry and ashamed,' he said. 'This is terrible girl, not keeping word. It is certainly because you give her such jolly good time, but I lose face greatly.'

'Don't feel like that, Mr Sombolon,' Pidduck said cheerfully. 'I know just how these things happen. So I suppose you'd better bring her round again tonight and I'll do my duty by the company and the export drive, eh?'

'You are truly great gentleman,' Mr Sombolon said, shifting from craven apologies to his more familiar style of fawning flattery. 'I bring her at eight, isn't it.'

As he made his way across the hotel lobby to the exit, his attention was drawn to a group of four Japanese in dark suits marching in line towards the reception desk, their suitcases borne by two porters. Mr Sombolon recognized the leading Japanese, a wizened septuagenerian named Mr Sanjiro Konoda, with a mouthful of decayed teeth. He was President of the Petroleum Supplies subsidiary of Kawama Industries. One of the bids temporarily mislaid by Mr Sombolon's cousin in the Ministry of Mines bore the name and oilrig symbol of Kawama and it was probably the lowest figure. 'We must move fast,' Mr Sombolon said to himself. 'Tonight the Englishman must perform well.' He watched from a distance as the four Japanese checked in at the desk, and as he left they were bowing to each other from the waist before making off to their various rooms. 'And where,' Mr Sombolon mused as he waited for a taxi, 'are the Americans? No doubt at the Hilton.' Their bid, also, was safely in his cousin's hands for a few more days.

CHAPTER
5

George Pidduck's second encounter with Hildegarde Glauber left him, for the first time in his life, with a dull ache in his lower back. He also had two perfect replicas of Hildegarde's front dentition in neat bloodshot marks on either shoulder. Lying contentedly next to him she had told him slowly and methodically, like the honourable girl she was, exactly what she had learned from the General. She had remembered it all.

'That is very good, Hildegarde,' Pidduck said. 'Very good indeed. Very useful. I would like you to get more information about all this if you can.'

'Okay, *mein Liebchen*,' she said. 'And in the bed I tell you, yes?'

'Sure, why not?'

'And we do more new things together?'

'I don't believe it!'

'Also you pay me dollars?'

'Yes. How much?'

'Fifteen hundred dollars US.' It was the figure already in her mind and it occupied all the limited space there, admitting of no other.

'All right,' Pidduck said, 'if you give me good information.'

'But that must you not tell to Sombolon,' Hildegarde said. 'To Sombolon you say I do it for love – no money, okay?'

'Okay. It's our little secret.'

Next morning over breakfast in the hotel's cafeteria, he told Mr Sombolon what Hildegarde had told him. 'It's a pretty smart move by the frogs,' he said.

'Very clever,' Mr Sombolon said, 'and we must do something more clever still.'

'Do you have any ideas?'

'Ideas for the moment, no. But respectfully I have questions.'

'Fire away.'

'Firstly, is this Legion of Honour truly very big honour in France?'

'Not all that big. If they give him the lowest rank – which is what I'd bet on – he'll be in there with a lot of provincial mayors and successful grocers. But I'm sure he doesn't know that now, and if we told him he'd never believe it.'

'And will it truly be given by French President in person?'

'I doubt it. I expect they'll tell him it will, get him to Paris and then claim the President has bursitis or something and hand him on to the Deputy Under-Secretary for Foreign Trade.'

'Does your great company have possibilities to stop this award? Maybe tell French Government bad things about General.'

'I'd have to think about that, but I doubt it. They've given it to worse crooks than him.'

'Then I will ask, can your great country offer better honours?'

Pidduck shook his head. 'Afraid not. It isn't that we're particularly fussy in that department. It's just that we aren't as flexible as the French – can't move fast enough.'

Mr Sombolon thought for a while. 'My thinkings,' he said at last, 'are respectfully these. General this time is minded for great honour, not great moneys. If he want moneys, boat, girls, he come always to us. "Sombolon," he says, "it is my pleasure this time to have this-that." And always he knows our great Company gives this-that. But now he will not speak any more with me because he wants to be big man in France, making ha-ha joke with President, getting this honour so when he returns to Jakarta he has gained much face with other Generals. Therefore,' Mr Sombolon continued, 'we also must make offerings which confer honour and much face. Those are my thinkings.'

'Christ,' Pidduck said, 'it's a tall order!'

'Please?'

'It's bloody difficult.'

'Indeed, yes.'

They sat in silence. 'Can you not give General big military decoration?' Mr Sombolon asked at last. 'I have heard of your Victoria Cross. I am told it is a very fine decoration. Is this not possible?'

Pidduck started to explain why the Victoria Cross was unlikely, at a week's notice, to be awarded to a corrupt Indonesian General of Engineers who wasn't even in his own country's army any longer, let alone Britain's. He found the cultural gap between the innocence of Mr Sombolon's question and the realities of British military awards too great to bridge. 'Just take my word for it,' he said lamely. 'It can't be done.'

'Or perhaps,' Mr Sombolon said after another pause, 'a high decoration in one of your colonies?'

Pidduck shook his head. 'There aren't many left, you know. And I don't think he'd go for something in Belize in preference to the Legion of Honour.'

'Excuse me, I do not know of Belize.'

They lapsed into silence again.

'You know,' Pidduck said at last, 'I need to soak myself a bit more in all this – get to know more about this bloody fellow's background, his tastes and habits. Is there anything written about him in English?

'A most excellent idea, Sir,' Mr Sombolon said. 'There is Entakan booklet with very friendly and favourable biography of General written by himself. Hotel book-stall has copies. Wait please.' He returned a few minutes later with a paperback which he handed to Pidduck. The title read: *The Story of Entakan and its Leader.* Pidduck glanced inside. There was plenty about General Nasturtion. 'Good,' he said, 'I'll read that later. How much longer have we got?'

'My cousin at Ministry of Mines tells me he must find

50

mislaid tenders in two days. Minister is very furious.'

'We'll need longer than that.'

'Maybe we get longer for 250 dollars US.'

'But we've already paid him 500 dollars and the time we bought isn't up yet.'

'My cousin says new situation makes big problems for him.'

'What new situation?'

'Very furious Minister.'

'All right, arrange it with Singapore.'

'Respectfully, Sir, already done,' Mr Sombolon said.

Later, Pidduck settled down with the fanciful official account of the foundation and growth of Entakan, Indonesia's premier company and virtually a state within the state. He read twice the account of General Nasturtion's early life, his studies in engineering, his entry into the army and his rapid rise to the General Staff before moving into Entakan to clear up the mess left by his predecessor. Through the breathless prose, one or two facts, or alleged facts, caught Pidduck's attention. He made some marks in the margins. Then he made some notes on a sheet of the hotel's letterhead:

1. Poor family – small farmers.
2. Made sacrifices for his education.
3. Secondary school and Jakarta University.
4. Left for army during troubles of 1952-3 without graduating. Allegedly out of patriotism – anti-communism.
5. Writes fondly of his humble family's sacrifices for him.
6. Turned Entakan to profit in 2 years.
7. Many military and civil decorations – seems to love them.

Pidduck sat staring at the list. Then he paced up and down his room and returned to the list. He did this several times. After an hour he had an idea. 'It might work,' he said to himself. 'It's all I can think of, anyway. I'll try it on Sombolon.' He put the book away and went down to the bar for a drink, passing the four Japanese in the lobby. Three of them were carrying cameras: they had been on an expedition to Ancol. They bowed in his direction as he went by and he had the uncomfortable feeling that they knew who he was.

When Mr Sombolon joined him, he outlined his plan. Mr Sombolon sat in silence for quite a while after he'd finished. He was pondering not one thing but two. Could the plan work? And if it worked, could it offer him any opportunities along the way to be of service and thus to earn some personal revenue? He came to the conclusion that it scored well for workability and quite fair for revenue. He decided to support it.

'A most brilliant thinking,' he told Pidduck at last. 'I am full of admirings for your ideas. I believe this may greatly interest General more than damn French plan. But may I ask respectfully, can you do this thing?'

'I think so. I'll call Papadopoulos in New York tonight and get him to work on it. He's a great fellow – very resourceful. We should know within forty-eight hours.'

A slow smile was spreading over Mr Sombolon's face. 'If we have this offering to make to the General, then is possible to say bad things about Legion of Honour. We say Legion is okay, sure, but, but, but . . . this here is much better. Oh, this is most excellent thinking by you.'

'You can say the French Government award about a thousand of them a year, so he'd be one of a thousand, among the grocers and champion bicyclists and officials who've reached retirement without being caught in a felony. Tell him the President makes very few of the awards himself. And make a particular point of the bicyclists in their yellow jerseys. But of course, you can't say any of that unless *he* tells *you* about the French offer. I don't want that girl put in any kind of danger, you understand.'

'Most certainly,' Mr Sombolon said, smiling. 'She is very fine woman and she has hots for you, isn't it.'

'Never mind that. What I want you to do now, Mr

Sombolon, is to get an interview with the General for tomorrow if you can, or the day after at latest. And then I want you to make this offer to him just as if it's already been fixed up. We'll take a chance on being able to deliver what we promise.'

'Absolutely good thinkings,' Mr Sombolon said, 'but you must instruct me, please, what I am to say to General.'

'I'll do that as soon as you've got your appointment, right?'

'Very good. I will use my excellent connections. Please now excuse me. I have many persons to see,' and he took his leave and felt his way out of the bar.

Pidduck finished his drink and went up to his room, where he put in a call to Nicos Papadopoulos, the Greek who was the All World man in the States. When it came through he spent ten minutes explaining what he wanted. 'You're crazy,' Papadopoulos said when he'd finished. 'Sure we can do it, but we'll never do it in the time.'

'You have to, Nicos. There's this sixteen-million-dollar contract riding on it and no one can sign with this little runt unless he gets what he wants. And this is what he'll want when we tell him about it.'

'What are the Japs and Yanks offering?'

'We don't know, but we think only we and the French are left in the game.'

'None of my business, George,' Papadopoulos said, 'but keep an eye over your left shoulder. There have to be other offers on the table.'

'Well, I can't afford to worry about what I don't know. I *do* know he's about to sign with the French and so that has to be my target. And that's why I need your help, Nicos my old buddy.'

'Okay, I'll do it for you. But don't beef if I fail. It looks like I'll have to get my knee into someone's groin really fast.'

'And who better than you to undertake subtle stuff like that?'

'Ah, shit. I'll call you when I have any news. You said I can go to a quarter of a million?'

'That's right.'

'And if it costs more?'

'Come back to me.'

'Okay. Goodbye now.'

If it could be done, Pidduck reflected as he climbed into bed, a cut-throat like Nicos would do it. He got into a position which was reasonably comfortable for his back and was soon asleep.

CHAPTER
6

A lifetime in the oil business in four continents had left Nicos Papadopoulos with a number of simple convictions about human nature to which he held with absolute certainty. One was that you'd better wear glasses or they'll steal your eyeballs. Another, that if every man had his price then some came dearer than others but none as dear as the incorruptible, who were very expensive indeed and therefore ended more corrupt than the rest. Also, he believed that it took an Armenian to deal with a Jew and an Anatolian Greek from Turkey to deal with a mainland Greek and a mainland Greek to deal with an Armenian, thus making the Anatolians (of which he was one) the greatest businessmen on earth (the Lebanese, he granted, had talent). And that there was better baklava to be had on the West Side in New York than anywhere in the Greek archipelago.

George Pidduck's request he regarded as little more than an irritant since for a quarter of a million dollars you could buy up and dispose of a lot of scruples. The only problem was time. He was a mountain of a man, the swarthy, tousled head sitting on a vast pear-shaped torso – the whole weighing a good 280 pounds without his Lobb shoes and the 8-ounce alpaca from Peruzzi of Rome. But though the body was of necessity slow, his mind moved at frightening speed. The twinkling, intelligent eyes were part of his great charm, and so was the boyish smile. Nicos was a most dangerous opponent and a most charming ally. The problem always was to know which side he was currently on and who, there-fore, he was currently screwing and for how much. From time to time one of the more pusillanimous members of the Board of All World in London, having heard that Nicos was believed to have made more for himself on a deal than he had made for the company he represented, would enquire plaintively whether it was fit and proper to continue employing a man who felt free to rob his employers in broad daylight, and whether opinion in the city might not be offended if it were to be known that . . . . At which point Rufus Pipe would growl across the board table at the doubter: 'Papa's the best man in the oil business in the whole of North America. How the hell do you expect anyone but an unprincipled ruffian to deal with the Americans and come away with his teeth still in his head? You gentlemen don't understand the business you're in.'

That would quieten the part-time directors for a while and Pipe would call the Greek and tell him to be a trifle more circumspect next time. 'My dear, dear Rufus,' Papadopoulos would gurgle into the telephone, 'what are you fussing about? Did we do the deal? Yes! Did we beat the piss out of the Yanks and the Japs? Yes! Also the Norwegians? Certainly! Did we make a nice profit? Yes! Could any of those pansies in London have done it? No! Only Nicos could do it. So leave me alone.' And a great chuckle would go out over the transatlantic cable and London would shut up for a while.

Now, he attacked the problem George Pidduck had set him. It was this: how in forty-eight hours to find a tolerably respectable and three-parts genuine American university willing to grant a Doctorate to an Indonesian General and to issue the invitation within the week, no questions asked. And since there was no good reason why any American institution of learning should grant a Ph.D. to an Indonesian ex-army businessman of whom they had probably never heard; and since General Nasturtion had on several public occasions made disobliging remarks about the United States and what he called its colonialist-racist-fascistic Government; and since, further, to the extent that he was known at all in the Western hemisphere he was known as the most

56

thoroughly corrupt man east of the Asian land mass; since all this, and much else, was so, Nicos Papadopoulos would have need of his quarter-million slush fund. With it he was to smooth out whatever academic scruples he might encounter, probably by offering to endow the university in question with a Chair, or maybe a couple of squash courts, a new cafeteria, or a psychiatric facility for faculty members, according to the needs of the moment and the tastes of the university President. Or maybe the money would be needed to pay off an impatient bank or a nasty accumulation of mortgage arrears. All he had to do was find the right institution — which meant an institution with an acute cash problem and a thoroughly worldly President. Given these two conditions, he knew he could swing it.

He called his friend Hank Butterworth, who held the Chair in Hydrocarbon Geology at the University of Illinois, and put the problem to him.

'The big guys are out,' the Professor said. 'Harvard and Princeton and that gang won't look at you. Nor would we: we're stuffed with auto money and our board's in recess for a month anyway.'

'Aren't the people in Texas the best bet?' Papadopoulos asked. 'They know all about oil.'

'Which means they'll know all about your guy, Nicos you fool. You need a bunch of ignorant bastards who've overspent their budget building some idiotic facility and will do anything to get out of hock because the newspapers are after them.'

'Is that hard to find, Hank?'

'Hell, no. All I have to do is call a friend of mine at the Ford Foundation and ask him who they've turned down lately and which of the rejects sounded hysterical. Give me an hour and I'll call you back.'

Professor Butterworth was true to his word. Forty minutes later he was on the line. 'No problem,' he said. 'My friend says the Foundation is being driven crazy by one Harvey Zimmerman who's the President of the University of Southern Arizona at Hackberry. He

57

checked with the Sloan-Kettering and Rockefeller people while I held. Apparently they've had this maniac after them too.'

'Thanks, Hank. Got the guy's number?'

Hank Butterworth had it and gave it to him. 'It's nothing,' he said. 'You can do me a favour some time.'

'Sure, sure,' Papadopoulos said. A plan of campaign was already forming in his mind. He dialled the number in Hackberry. An exceedingly languorous voice from somewhere below the Mason-Dixon line answered. 'President Zimmerman's office. This is Suzie taking your call.'

'Hallo, Suzie,' Papadopoulos said. 'How are you?'

'I'm just great, thank you. And how're you-all?' She sounded as if she greatly wanted to know.

'I'm fine, Suzie.' He wondered if the telephone system had switched him to the Hackberry Massage Parlour in error. It couldn't be, he decided. They'd be far more businesslike there. 'I'd like to speak with President Zimmerman,' he said.

'Who shall I say?'

'Say Nicos Papadopoulos of the All World Foundation. Say I'd like to talk about some funding for the University.'

'Let me get that.' She struggled with his name and finally got it right. 'That's a cute name,' she said.

'It's Greek – Nicos Papadopoulos.'

'Now isn't that *something*,' she said. 'That really gets to me.' She allowed his name to gurgle and sigh up from her throat like a long-distance embrace.

'What the hell *is* this,' Papadopoulos asked himself. 'What kind of a University President can let a kook like this take his calls?' To Suzie, gurgling into the Bell System a thousand miles away, he said: 'I'm glad you like my name, Suzie. So what do you say, shall we get the President now?'

'Why surely,' Suzie said. 'Tell you what I'll do. I'll put you on hold and I'll tell the President Mr Nicos Papadopoulos is calling him long-distance about some funding. Does that mean cash?'

'It could mean cash.'

'Why, the President will just love that. So you just hold, rightie?'

'Rightie.'

He was switched, surprisingly, to a recording of J.S. Bach on the unaccompanied cello. 'Oh, Mr Papadopoulos,' Suzie said a minute later, cutting into an andante of surpassing beauty, 'let me pass you to the President now, and I just want to say at this time that it was a real pleasure talking to you.'

'Thanks, Suzie,' Papadopoulos said. 'It was my pleasure.' He thought the woman must be crazy. With J.S. Bach and Suzie disposed of, he awaited President Zimmerman.

The President's voice proved to be quite different from everything that had gone before. A whole new culture. 'Yeah,' he said.

'Good day to you, President,' Papadopoulos said. 'I am Nicos Papadopoulos and I represent the interests of the All World Foundation in the United States.'

'Never heard of it,' the President said, 'and I thought I knew all the Foundations.' He had a voice like an ill-adjusted buzz-saw. It was the voice of a man who had wandered into the deserts of Arizona from a more urbanized and harsher environment. A city voice.

'We're a British-based outfit,' Papadopoulos said. 'Our money comes from industrial activities in the area of hydrocarbon research, exploitation and servicing.'

'You mean the oil business or the coal business?'

'I mean the petroleum industry,' Papadopoulos said. He was determined to sound academic, just as President Zimmerman was determined to sound like a businessman.

'You a Greek?' the President asked.

'I am.'

'We do Greek studies here – history, archeology, stuff like that.'

'I see.'

59

'And we're very strong on the environment – ecology, the no-osphere, the way mankind's beating the shit out of its own resources, you know? My predecessor accepted a lot of dough from a nut who'd made it big in female deodorants and decided he'd wrecked mankind's future with all that gas from his aerosols floating up and burning holes in the ozone layer. So he funded a whole department here and we've been overrun with ecology weirdos ever since.'

'I understand. It sounds very relevant. Could tie in nicely with our own interests – energy resource preservation and so on.'

'I'm reading you, Nicos. That's great thinking,' the President said. 'So what can I do for you?'

'I have a proposition I'd like to discuss with you.'

'You got a funding project?'

'We may have. Only we need to move very fast. Owing to an oversight not of our making we have certain funds which must be allocated by next week. That's required under the terms of our trust deed.' Papadopoulos had run himself in and was now lying fluently.

'Yeah, and why us?' For a man said to be in desperate need of money, President Zimmerman was playing it real cool.

'Your University was recommended to us. Possibly because of your work on ecology.'

'How much dough?'

'That's something I'd prefer to discuss round the table. I was going to suggest that I fly out to meet with you. Say tomorrow?'

'That's great, Nicos. I'd planned a little golf but I can stall that. You know how to get to this god-forsaken hole?'

'No, but I'll get my secretary to work things out with yours.'

'Tell her to ask for Suzie.'

'I'll do that. Goodbye.'

'Take care.'

60

Papadopoulos was met at the undersized Flagstaff airport by Suzie. He had flown in by DC6 on the feeder line from Phoenix with a load of tourists heading for that vast geological blunder, the Grand Canyon. Suzie had dazzled the airport staff into letting her drive an enormous Buick convertible onto the apron, so that Papadopoulos was confronted with her and the car as he lowered his great bulk down the steps from the aircraft.

Her telephone voice had been no confidence trick. What it promised electronically the reality duly delivered. Everything was there – the mane of shining blonde hair, the tip-tilted peaches-and-cream Southern prettiness, the milk-fed body with the American breasts, the mix of sparkling health and sexual languor which seemed to be a principal outcome of the American system of higher education – all this encased in a pair of hotpants which had been painted onto her, and a top from which her breasts were trying to escape.

She waved, selecting him easily from among the holiday crowd in their double-knit synthetics. 'Hiya,' she said. 'I'm Suzie.'

'Nice of you to meet me, Suzie,' Papadopoulos said. He shook her hand and climbed into the car beside her. She waved to the leering ground staff and drove the Buick out of the airport and onto the highway.

'They were just great, letting me in there like that,' she said. 'Don't you think people are really great?'

'Sure, great,' Papadopoulos said. Suzie's propositions, delivered with awesome confidence, were all sweeping – vast in their scope and devoid of escape clauses. 'Some of them,' he added.

'*I* think people are simply great.' That was her position on the people question.

She drove the big car with style and confidence. Papadopoulos glanced speculatively at her, observing her splendid bosom in profile and being rewarded with a sudden turn of the golden head and a flashing smile. 'As I thought – perfect teeth,' he said to himself. 'She

61

isn't real.'

'So you're President Zimmerman's secretary,' he said.

'I'm the President's Executive Assistant,' Suzie said.

'Do you like that?'

'It's a terrific job. Mr Zimmerman's a simply terrific human being. He's very, very dynamic. I think dynamic people are great.'

Papadopoulos could think of no way to respond to Suzie on dynamism.

'He's a Leo,' she said. 'You-all a Leo?'

'I don't know, Suzie.'

'You don't *know* your *sign*? You kidding me?'

'I'm not. I just don't know.'

'You simply unglue me. What's your birth date?'

'August ten.'

'You're a Leo,' she cried triumphantly. 'I simply *love* Leos. They're such *successful* people. President Zimmerman is a very, very successful person. He's done lots of wonderful things for the University since he became President.'

'When was that, Suzie?'

'About two years ago, I guess.'

'And how long have you been his Executive Assistant?'

'About a year. I was a student, you know, planning to major in Women's Rights. That and Apartment Management. Then the President said why did I want to bother my head with all that stuff, you know, when there were better ways, like, for me to fulfil myself. And as I think fulfilment is very, very important, I said okay I'd drop my course and move into his office. Don't you think that was a wonderful thing for the President to do? You see, he's very people-oriented.'

They were driving through the scrub and rock of a blistering, desolate landscape. Once the road took them through a dead mining town, abandoned when the mines gave out half a century ago. The gap-toothed rows of derelict shacks and houses looked like a carefully wrecked back-lot at Universal. The mine workings on the

62

hillside were like abstracts of rusted ironwork and rotting timber from an avant-garde sculpture show. The air was dry and hot in their faces. Suzie chattered amiably, her propositions defying all comment.

The campus at Hackberry proved to be a great sprawl of Spanish-style buildings like some endless hacienda. They were set amidst irrigated lawns and flower beds and were liberally festooned with wrought iron gates, window grilles, balustrades and lamp brackets. The place was cluttered with ill-clad students. Suzie nosed the car along the driveway past clumps of hairy young people, waving here and there, and brought it to a stop before a three-storey building. A legend in ironwork mounted on a stone plinth proclaimed ADMINISTRATION BLOCK.

'We made it,' she said to Papadopoulos. 'President Zimmerman will be waiting for you.' She led him down cool corridors to a door marked OFFICE OF THE PRESIDENT. She opened it without knocking. 'I've brought Mr Papadopoulos, honey,' she said. 'Can he come on in?'

'Sure, bring him in,' said a voice.

President Zimmerman proved to be small and deeply tanned, with a mass of grey hair which had been carefully randomized across his scalp and over his ears. He advanced briskly towards Papadopoulos, who noticed that in his elevator shoes the President reached to Suzie's chin – perhaps to her clavicle if his hair were flattened, and to her shoulder without the shoes. He flashed a good deal of gold about his person – a chain around his neck with a heavy charm flopping against his abdomen, an identity bracelet on one wrist and a gold and gold-strapped watch on the other. He also wore a lot of rings. His check Dacron golfing slacks were topped by a Lacoste short-sleeved shirt in blinding white. Papadopoulos thought he had the face of a Miami real estate broker. What on earth could such a man be doing out here in the desert, masquerading as an academic bureaucrat? Perhaps it took men like this to raise and administer the vast funds needed to keep

63

the sprinklers going in these elaborate private institutions of learning.

'Sit down,' President Zimmerman commanded, 'and have a drink. I'm drinking Jack Daniels.' He trotted to the far corner of the room where armchairs had been arranged around a low coffee table. 'What's yours?'

'The same, thank you. Straight on the rocks,' Papadopoulos said.

'Suzie, honey,' President Zimmerman said, 'fix that, will you?'

'Why, surely,' Suzie said. She busied herself at a French escritoire which stood against a wall and which looked genuine. It had been transformed into a cocktail cabinet. She prepared the drinks, mixed herself a Bloody Mary and joined them around the table.

'I'm listening,' President Zimmerman said. 'What's on your mind, Nicos?'

Papadopoulos went through the story he had prepared, stopping short once he had revealed that All World had a quarter of a million dollars which had to be found a home by the following week. He made no mention of General Nasturtion. While he talked, President Zimmerman drummed his fingers on the arm of his chair. He was clearly a man who preferred talking to listening, even when what he heard was dollars and cents.

'Yeah,' he said when Papadopoulos judged that a pause would be appropriate. 'Yeah, we could probably help you out with your little problem, Nicos. I can see a positive way to put that kind of money to work, can't you, Suzie?'

'I sure can,' Suzie said. 'Very positive.'

'You see what Nicos is driving at,' Zimmerman explained, as to a child. 'They have all this dough burning a hole in their pants, right, and they need a project that can mop it up.'

'That certainly seems to be their problem,' Suzie said. 'I see that.'

President Zimmerman's eyes narrowed. 'How fussy

do you people get after the dough's been placed?' he asked Papadopoulos. 'You come crawling all over us here, making audits and crap like that?'

Papadopoulos waved an expressive hand and treated the President to his sunniest smile. 'Well, we're answerable to the trustees for the funding we do, so naturally we have to be interested in how the money's being used. There's a reporting procedure – the usual kind of thing, you understand.'

'Your trustees British?'

'Yes.'

'They stay in Britain or do they come nosing around all over the damn place?'

'Generally, they stay over there and take my word for the fact that the funds aren't being misapplied.'

The President nodded and his eyes narrowed still further. 'You the key guy in this transaction, right?'

'You could say that,' Papadopoulos said, adopting an expression he had had occasion to use in such circumstances before. It said, *I know you think I'm bribable and you're looking for a way to do it, so just try me: it isn't difficult and you'll find I know how to conduct conversations of this kind.*

'Honey,' President Zimmerman said suddenly to Suzie, 'why don't you do those calls for me while I finish this thing with Nicos?'

'What calls?' Suzie asked.

'Why, those calls I asked you to make yesterday.'

'Oh, *those* calls.' She had connected.

'Yeah, those,' said the President.

'Rightie,' she said and swayed out of the room with incredible erotic meaning.

'A great girl,' the President said. 'A great Executive Assistant. The best I ever had. Except that she can never remember a damn thing.'

Papadopoulos sipped at his drink and settled back comfortably in his chair. The conversation was shaping nicely. He awaited President Zimmerman's next remark with the confidence of a man who is about to be offered money.

65

'How much?' the President barked at him now they were alone.

Papadopoulos was used to subtler stuff than this but he did not betray the fact. 'You realise it would be both difficult and dangerous for me to overlook what the University was doing with our money,' he said.

'And I wouldn't ask you to, Nicos, I wouldn't ask you to. It's just that I haven't time to answer a lot of damn fool questions and shepherd a bunch of stupid limeys round the place every five minutes.'

'I understand perfectly. My problem is that we have a very difficult Chairman back in London. The only way I could keep him away from this is by telling him the University insists on privacy, and knowing this is a little, er, unorthodox, they are prepared to make a donation to any cause or charity nominated by him. It might be the World Wildlife Fund or maybe a home for indigent gentlefolk he's interested in or something to do with cats.'

'Cats?'

'Yes, he's very fond of cats.'

'Christ,' the President said.

'It's the kind of thing he's accepted in similar circumstances,' Papadopoulos said, 'so I know he'll buy it.'

'So how much?' The President said it like a man who's heard a few in his time, including this one.

'Say fifty thousand dollars and a favour which would cost you nothing.'

President Zimmerman gave a fair imitation of a man stung by a bee.

'That's *crazy*,' he shouted, his eyes open wide now, lest more were to be stolen from him. 'Why that's twenty per cent of the goddamn money, Nicos. You can't expect that much.'

'Not me,' Papadopoulos said gently. 'Our chairman in London.'

'You, the chairman, what do I care? It's goddamn robbery.'

66

'It's the only way,' Papadopoulos said, 'unless you want three-monthly audits. And there's the favour.'

'Christ,' the President said again, 'd'you want the shirt off my back as well?'

'The favour is very important.'

'So what the hell is it?'

Papadopoulos explained carefully the case of General Nasturtion, omitting everything he deemed to be a distraction and adding a certain amount of what seemed to him useful and persuasive detail.

'We have a committee of faculty members to settle these things,' the President said. 'I'll call 'em in this afternoon and we can fix it on the spot. They eat out of my hand.'

'That's fine.'

'But fifty grand, for God's sake. Listen, Nicos, don't crucify me like this. Come on, make nice and I'll throw in a couple of Ph.D's for anyone else you fellows care to nominate.,'

'Sorry, but our position isn't negotiable.'

'But twenty per cent for God's sake. Five per cent I heard of. Even seven and a half. But I *never* heard of twenty.'

'Our Chairman is not a small-minded man, President.'

'Call me Harvey,' the President said gloomily.

'I, too, think twenty per cent is high, Harvey, but what can we poor intermediaries do – you on behalf of this great University, I on behalf of the Foundation?'

'Great University my tits,' the President rasped. 'The place is a goddamn home for weirdos, dope-heads, commies and homosexuals. Listen, I was in the dry goods business in Phoenix before I came out here. Just like Goldwater, and he moved to the US Senate and tried for the White House. Don't ask me why I made the move but times were tough in dry goods and I saw great business possibilities here. Mind you, we were grossing four million a year and netting close to a quarter of a million, so I wasn't on any damn breadline.

When I'm asked what line I'm in now I say I'm in the communications business because that's what a University is. That and real estate. You see, the University owns a lot of prime land in this part of the State and I've got the Board of Regents to release some of it for development under my control. The mortgagors are driving us out of our skulls right now but it's going to pay nicely.' He didn't say who would be paid and Papadopoulos didn't ask him.

'In dry goods,' President Zimmerman continued, 'we work on a forty per cent margin, reckon to turn our stock twice a year, and achieve a decent cash flow by letting our suppliers scream for their money until they throw up. But here it's another ball of wax. Business principles are very, very difficult to apply. It's one hell of an uphill struggle.'

'I can believe it.'

'Our cash flow here stinks, I can tell you. I've got a dozen economists in the joint, including a Professor of Applied Economics, and between them they can't make two dollars and two dollars come to four dollars. As soon as it's dollars they act like women. Four of 'em *are* women. Jesus, they count on their *fingers!*'

Papadopoulos nodded sympathetically.

'Listen,' the President snarled, 'I'm trying to run a business here. A lousy business giving a lousy return on the invested funds, but still a business.'

'But what about the students? I see students here. Don't you turn out graduates?'

'Oh, those assholes,' he said savagely. 'Place would be far better off without them. I admit some of the chicks are cute. Suzie was on a course on socially-oriented developments in the women's movement or some such crap. I pulled her out of there and gave her this job as my Executive Assistant. A cute chick. But as for the men – asshole each and every one.' President Zimmerman finished his drink and grabbed at the whiskey bottle. 'It's the bottom line that counts,' he snapped. 'What's the use of turning out a lot of shitty graduates in

Interpersonal Motivation or whatever the hell it is, if the bottom line's printed in red? Tell me that.'

'No point at all. And I hope our little contribution may help.'

'Make the kicker twenty-five,' Zimmerman said.

Papadopoulos beamed at him and shook his head. He had his man in a half-nelson and he wasn't one to throw victory away. 'Sorry, Harvey, can't do.'

'You're killing me,' Zimmerman said. 'You're affecting my mental health.'

'I'm giving you two hundred thousand bucks, net, and very few questions asked.'

'Look, Nicos, my broker's making margin calls day and night. Talk to me, Nicos, baby. Can't you screw a few grand more out of those limeys?'

Papadopoulos shook his head again.

'When can I have the money?'

'Well, once your committee has agreed to the General's Ph.D and I've told London, they'll transfer the money through their bank, payable after the investing ceremony. I guess that could be within a month.'

The President screwed his face up in a look of distaste. 'I – we could use the money sooner than that. We have some big payments to make on the 30th.'

'Sorry, I don't see how we can work much faster. And as for the chairman's donation, he leaves the mechanics of that entirely to me. You see, he likes these donations to be made in his own name.'

'So the pussy-cats will know where the money comes from,' Zimmerman said sourly.

'That kind of thing. Anyway, for that to happen we have to handle cash, you understand.'

'I wasn't planning to do it on my credit card.' The President hadn't got over his bitterness at the fifty thousand.

Papadopoulos ignored him. 'So I'll collect the Chairman's money in cash at the same time as we release the funds from the bank. Meanwhile, I'll be drawing up a simple agreement between us that I'll be asking you to sign. It's no big deal.'

The President looked wary. 'And do I get a receipt for the fifty grand?'

'No, sir.'

'So I'm vulnerable if anyone comes nosing around, right?'

'That, I'm afraid, is your problem. But certainly *we* shan't be nosing around.'

'Wouldn't be healthy with the fifty grand under your belt,' the President said.

'Not *my* belt,' Papadopoulos explained patiently. 'Whales, old gentlefolk, pussy cats.'

President Zimmerman grunted and got up. 'I suppose it's a deal,' he said. 'A lousy deal, but a deal. Now let's grab some food. We'll collect Suzie on the way, then she can run you back to make your flight.' As he trotted next to Papadopoulos along the corridor he was shaking his head. 'Twenty per cent,' he muttered. 'Who ever heard of twenty per cent?'

Late that night Papadopoulos called George Pidduck in Jakarta. 'I think I have what you want, George,' he said, 'but it looks like costing more than we hoped.'

'Good, Nicos, but how much more?'

'Fifty grand.'

Pidduck whistled. 'That much?'

'Afraid so. I've fixed the University for two-fifty but the President has to be squared personally. The thing offends against his academic standards or something. So we have to look after him outside the deal.'

'He comes expensive,' Pidduck said.

'He's a very tough nut.'

'Well,' Pidduck said, 'if that's what we have to do I suppose we'd better do it. I'll confirm the whole thing to you one way or the other within forty-eight hours. Sombolon is seeing our friend tomorrow. And meanwhile, thanks a lot, Nicos. It was wonderfully helpful.'

'What are friends for?' Papadopoulos said.

It was another of his maxims: make both sides pay. This time to the soothing music of one hundred thousand dollars in all.

CHAPTER
7

George Pidduck gave Mr Sombolon the news from
Arizona a few hours before the time fixed for the
meeting with General Nasturtion. Mr Sombolon had
obtained the interview by means of a modest but not
altogether unprincipled subterfuge. 'Tell your master,'
he had said to the General's secretary, 'that I have
important news from Germany which I feel should be
conveyed in person. I am at his disposal any time, day
or night.' The General had fixed the meeting for the
following day, and Pidduck and Mr Sombolon had used
the intervening time to some purpose. There had been
telephone conversations at length with the All World
office in Paris and with Sandy Macarthur in Singapore.
Fully briefed, Mr Sombolon now sat on the far side of
the General's enormous desk in a posture conveying a
careful mix of fawning servility and collusive chummi-
ness.

'So what is your news from Germany?' the General
asked without looking up from a document on his
blotter. 'No trouble with the three new girls, eh
Sombolon?'

'Allah be praised, none,' Mr Sombolon said. 'The
news in fact is good and may be greatly to your taste.'

'So what is it?'

'Of course, every man has his own ideas in such
matters, and I apologise most abjectly in advance if what
I have to tell you should prove not to be to your
taste . . .'

'Yes, yes,' the General said. 'I am a man of the world,
Sombolon, and nothing you can suggest in such matters
will offend me. So now tell me and stop wasting words.
I am very busy.'

'I do not wish to take up your time. I will therefore tell you. The three German girls you asked for some weeks ago have now been found and are on their way. They are truly exquisite creatures from the highest ranks of society and their measurements are as specified by you. Perhaps even a shade more generous.' He paused.

'Is that what you have to tell me?' the General asked.

'That, and also a further fact.'

'So?'

'The fact is that two of them are sisters. Twins – identical twins, I am told. I am also told some men would find such an arrangement – interesting.' He paused again and waggled a finger to convey he knew not what sexual delights. The General looked up and caught the stony glance of President Sokarno, looking down from a large frame on the wall behind Mr Sombolon's head. But his mind was not on that charismatic figure. He was pondering the possible effects of having his very specific requirements tended to by a couple of identical, heavy-buttocked siblings instead of by Hildegarde or Anneliese or Trudi or any of the others, acting alone. It had, he decided, definite erotic possibilities.

'Yes,' he said, 'that could be of interest. You have done well, Sombolon. When will they arrive?'

'Next week, General.'

'Good. Keep me informed.' He returned to the papers before him. The crucial moment had arrived. Mr Sombolon had not rushed matters: such things had to grow subtly out of a carefully orchestrated dialogue. And there was a right moment and a wrong one to switch the direction of such a conversation from one path onto another. Too soon, and you failed because your interlocutor was not yet ready. Too late, and you failed again because the moment of truth had been missed and his mind was detached from you and fastened onto other things. Now, Mr Sombolon decided, was the moment of truth. 'Please forgive me,' he said, and paused.

The General looked up. 'What is it now, Sombolon?'

'I have a modest favour to ask.'

'Yes, yes, what is it?'

'My British company has asked my opinion on an offer they had considered making to you, but I am a modest man with no pretensions to know your views on such questions. I am therefore presuming to ask you what reply to give to the Englishmen.'

'If this is in connection with the servicing contract, Sombolon, I am not interested. I intend to place it elsewhere this time.'

'That I understand. It is said the Japanese will get it.' Mr Sombolon was fishing. He felt a tug on the line.

'Nonsense. I intend to deal with the French.'

Mr Sombolon affected astonishment. His eyes opened wide and he raised his bony shoulders in an expressive gesture. 'The French?' he said. 'I trust they can offer . . . everything that is required.'

'They can indeed,' General Nasturtion said. 'What they have to offer is most satisfactory.'

'Can one enquire . . .'

'One can not enquire,' the General said. 'Now tell me what you want to know.'

'It is this, General,' Mr Sombolon said, speaking slowly so that the full implications of what he had to say should be properly absorbed. 'Our company, as you will know, does extensive business in the United States. Through our connections there we have been asked to nominate a distinguished personage of our choice in the oil industry to be honoured with the exceptional award of an honorary Doctorate – a Ph.D. – by one of the very leading universities there. Now, our Singapore office wish to nominate a well-known figure in the Malaysian oil industry whose name I am not at liberty to divulge. But when I heard of this I said to my Director in London: "This is absolutely preposterous. For do we not have as one of our most distinguished, important and cherished customers General Nasturtion of

73

Entakan? And would it not be a shameful insult to such a man not to make our first offer of this unique honour to him?" And my Director in London said: "But would the General be interested in a Ph.D. from a top American university? How would he feel, for instance, about the extensive publicity surrounding the award? For he must know that the Americans are crazy on publicity and his picture and biography would most certainly be published in the *New York Times* and *Newsweek* and *Time*, and all this would be reproduced by all the leading journals in Europe. And do we know that the General would be willing to submit himself to television and radio interviews as well?" And I replied; "I frankly do not know the answers to these questions." Then my Director said: "But is there not a further problem, since you tell us that this year we are not to be honoured with the Entakan contract? Does this not mean that in the General's eyes we are no longer a favoured supplier? So would it not offend him to receive this offer? For it might look as if we would not have made it had we not heard of the possible loss of the contract." This, you see, is how these Westerners reason. And so I replied: "Sombolon does not know the answer to your question but he will find out." And so I am humbly seeking your advice and apologizing if I am causing any offence.'

He brought his speech to an end with a small bow. He felt it had possessed the required ingredients: an unfolding narrative with a measure of suspense, a necessary element of respect, and above all the shrewd introduction of Malaysia. Like many Indonesians, General Nasturtion had no time at all for his country's neighbour across the straits. He could be relied upon to choke on the thought of any honour that might have been his going instead to a Malaysian. The General looked again at Sokarno. Then he looked down at Mr Sombolon, sitting diffident and humble before him.

'Harvard?' he asked.

'No, General.'

'Yale?'

'No.'

'Princeton or MIT?'

Mr Sombolon felt that the operation was getting away from him. 'Certainly not, General. These places are not highly regarded in our industry. The important degrees, carrying genuine prestige, come from the universities of the western United States.'

'So which one is it?'

'I am not at liberty to divulge the name, but in confidence I will nevertheless tell you. It is the most important of all the institutions producing graduates in our field – the University of Southern Arizona. You will surely have heard of them and their work on energy conservation?'

The General had not but did not care to admit it. 'Of course,' he said, and fell silent again. 'Someone in Malaysia, you said?'

Mr Sombolon nodded. 'I fear so,' he replied. He allowed a look of disgust to spread over his features.

'Who?'

'I am not at liberty to say, but it is Rahman of the National Oil Consortium.'

'A useless buffoon,' the General said.

'Undoubtedly,' Mr Sombolon agreed.

'So you want to know what I would think of such an offer for myself?' the General asked.

'That is my humble request.'

The General seemed to take a decision. 'Tell me this,' he said, 'have you heard of the French Legion of Honour?'

'Of course,' Mr Sombolon said, not believing his luck. It was now that he produced what he later described to his brother as his masterstroke. 'It is most certainly a very prestigious decoration,' he said. 'This must be so because I heard only last week that it had been offered to the Malaysian Minister of Defence following the sale to Malaysia of two French training aircraft. It was only a small sale, of course, and I understand the French

75

Government maintains a supply of these decorations to reward those who trade with French companies on a modest scale. They find it cheaper, of course, than other marks of gratitude for services rendered.' He paused for effect. Then he delivered a postscript. 'I believe they also give it to all their ambassadors and to their civil servants when they retire. If they award it so often it must be a very popular decoration.'

The General was staring hard at Mr Sombolon. He appeared to be wrestling with very powerful emotions. 'Are you sure of all this, Sombolon?'

'Indeed, I am, General,' said Mr Sombolon happily, piling Pelion on Ossa, though he was unaware of either. 'As a matter of fact, I remember that when I had the privilege to visit my Company in Europe and spend some days in Paris on my way back, I noticed in the Metro and other public places how many people were wearing these little red rosettes. I enquired about their significance and I was told that this was the highly popular French decoration, the Legion of Honour.'

A hard and dangerous look had come into the General's eyes. Set, as they were, close together, and glinting dangerously in this way, they made him look uncomfortably like a cornered and angry stoat. 'I see,' he said grimly. 'Is that really so?' He brought a hard brown fist down onto his blotter, making pens and ashtrays jump about on his desk. In the presence of unseemly anger, Mr Sombolon kept his eyes averted. The General might be a great and powerful man and wealthy beyond imagining, but Mr Sombolon now felt that he was leading him as one leads a bullock with a ring through its nose. He tugged gently on the ring.

'All this,' he said, 'is probably not known, of course, to the Malaysian fool who accepted the Legion of Honour as a reward for the trainer contract. The Malaysians do not understand the devious and unprincipled behaviour of Westerners as we do in Indonesia.'

The General was hardly listening, but the gist of this needling remark got through to him. 'Tell me, Sombolon,' he said, regaining control of his feelings, 'this Ph.D. which is offered, I might be interested in it. I believe I would be a very suitable recipient in view of my work here.' He waved an arm to encompass Entakan and its endless proliferations. 'Would your company be seriously interested in putting my name forward?'

'Indeed, they would if I speak to them,' Mr Sombolon said, allowing joy to be writ large across his expressive features. 'It would be the greatest honour imaginable to me to be allowed to act as intermediary in such a noble transaction.'

'I would require an official invitation from the head of the University', the General said.

'It can be arranged within a week.'

'And I would expect to travel to the ceremony as the guest of the University.'

'Of the company,' Mr Sombolon murmured, inserting the commercial *quid pro quo* deftly into the discussion. 'Our company would of course arrange all transport and accommodations for you and your suite. Perhaps your wife and children . . . to see you invested with your Doctorate?'

'Perhaps. My wife has wished for a long time to return to the United States on a visit. But she goes shopping there and her tastes are expensive. Also, our currency regulations . . .'

'No problem,' Mr Sombolon said. 'Our company will naturally look after all such matters.'

'Good.' The General got up to signify that the interview was at an end. Mr Sombolon rose and bowed low. 'I will report our conversation to our Director,' he said. 'I feel certain that this will put an end to the foolish Malaysian plan.'

'I trust so,' the General said.

As Mr Sombolon reached the door and turned for a final bow, the General made a pretence of suddenly recalling something. It did not fool Mr Sombolon and the General didn't expect it to. 'By the way, Sombolon,' he said, 'what was the name of that boatyard in Italy?'

'Davani of Genoa,' Mr Sombolon said. 'Naturally, we are still happy to . . .'

'Yes, yes,' the General said. 'We will have occasion to talk further about that matter. I hadn't forgotten it.'

'I am honoured.'

'Your tender is in, of course?'

'Of course, General.' Mr Sombolon took his leave.

That evening the General said to Hildegarde. 'I am not going to Paris after all.'

'*Ach, so,*' Hildegarde said, pausing for a moment as she manipulated her rubber tubes and nozzles and the big container of warm water. 'Why not, *mein Nasty?*'

'Ow, be careful,' the General said as a long plastic nozzle was inserted into his person. 'There, that is better. Further, please. Further, Ah!' He paused to contemplate the pleasure to come. 'I am going instead to the United States.'

'With your big Hilde, *ja?*'

'No. It isn't possible. Ah, that is very good.' What to most others would be an undignified and uncomfortable procedure had become for the General an essential concomitant of sexual bliss. He had discovered high colonics at the hands of a highly specialized whore in Manila and had not been the same man since. Once it had been established that this was a service which his wife was not prepared to render him, he had further refined and deepened the experience by having it administered by this plump German blonde in her boots and helmet. Now, as the water began to fill him up, he sighed deeply and let his mind dwell on the even plumper siblings who were said to be on their way from some corner of Germany. How had that fellow Sombolon found them, he wondered. A very resourceful type. Useful.

'The damned Frenchmen were trying to fool me,' he said to Hildegarde, 'but I saw through their game in no time. Let it flow quicker.'

'*Ja, ja.*' Hildegarde was thinking as fast as she was able. It was not fast by others' standards; only by her

78

own. After a long moment she said, 'So your contract to the Americans will be given?'

'No,' the General said. 'I have not decided yet. The Britishers think they will get it, but maybe yes, maybe no. Oh, oh, that is very fine. Is there more water to come?'

'*Ja*, a little.'

'Good, let it flow. I will see the Japanese and the Americans. I am smarter than these people. I play them off against each other. Maybe the Britishers will not get the contract after all.'

'*Das ist alles*,' Hildegarde said. 'All the water in you is flown.' She was busy storing these precious shards in her mind and inadvertently pushed at the nozzle instead of pulling.

'My God,' shrieked the General. 'You hurt me, you adorable creature. Do it again . . . please do it again.'

Hildegarde shrugged. If that was what the man wanted, that was what she would do for him, though she would never understand why. She grasped the base of the nozzle in her ample fist and shoved hard. It dug deep into the General. 'Oh, oh, oh, such bliss,' he moaned. But Hildegarde was thinking of the fascinating Englishman and his incredible endurance. She had fresh information for him and he would be pleased with her.

General Nasturtion's decision to accept an honorary Doctorate of Philosophy at the University of Southern Arizona at Hackberry produced repercussions in six cities, not counting Hackberry itself. It was as if a handful of pebbles had been flung into the still waters of a pool, the circling ripples spreading out, overlapping and interacting on each other. And at the centre of it all – the man who had flung the pebbles – sat George Pidduck, doing what he did well: organizing a corrupt and complex deal in the face of fierce and unprincipled competition.

First move was made by the General himself in Jakarta. He did a simple thing: he called a press conference and told the newspapermen that he would be going shortly to the USA to receive the highest academic honour that lay within their power to bestow – an Honorary Ph.D. at a leading American university. He made it clear at the same time that any editor who put the announcement inside his newspaper would be in heavy trouble. 'It is important front-page news,' he said. 'An honour, through me, for our country. I will therefore regard as unpatriotic anyone who fails to present it accordingly. Our press lacks ideology and respect for our country's leaders. So watch out.' He then posed for a fresh picture though the papers' photo libraries were stuffed with shots of him. He also demanded and obtained an interview on television and told the viewers that this award recognized the fact that he had sacrificed the last years of his own higher education to the noble cause of destroying communist subversion. This, he said, was recognized by the Americans and was the inner significance of the event. To himself he said, 'With all this publicity the devious and untrustworthy British will be unable to back out.'

While the General was seen posturing on the television screen in his hotel room, Pidduck was frantically phoning New York. 'The news is out, I couldn't stop it,' he told Papadopoulos. 'You've got to harden the whole thing up, Nicos, and get an official invitation out of this President of yours right away – tomorrow latest.'

'No problem,' Papadopoulos said soothingly. 'He'll play. Don't forget, he's bought. When you own them they play.'

'I'm fixing the details of that side of things,' Pidduck said. 'The necessary will come into your special account from Sandy in Singapore, using Barclays for the transfer.'

'Don't forget the guy's extra fifty,' Papadopoulos said, very willing to oblige but ever watchful for his own interests.

'It hurts but I won't.'

They fixed dates for the visit and other details that Mr Sombolon had obtained from the General's private office. There would be fifteen people in the official party. It would mean chartering a plane from Phoenix and a fleet of limousines to take them on to Hackberry.

In Paris, at the headquarters of Bernard de Brives de Moustier's company, the excessive and premature euphoria of the past fortnight gave way to a Gallic mixture of gloom, astonishment and blind fury. In room 606 in Jakarta the small and now despondent Frenchman sat by the telephone and tried to explain what had gone wrong. He had discovered George Pidduck's identity, and his sense of betrayal and personal failure knew no bounds.

'Perfidious Albion,' he moaned into the mouthpiece.

'Be less poetic and more concrete,' snapped his Chairman from Paris. 'What the devil happened?'

'I do not know. I simply don't understand it,' de Brives de Moustier wailed. 'I had everything fixed, and then on his return from Riau the General refused to see me. The next I knew was this press announcement, and the rumour in Jakarta is that it was all fixed by the British and they will get the contract again.'

'We should have kept those lousy swine out of the Common Market,' his Chairman said.

'It would not have helped in this instance,' de Brives de Moustier pointed out.

'Don't argue with me, damn you.' The Chairman, always testy, was audibly livid with rage. 'Just stay there and try to restore the situation. Do something. See the embassy. Use your brains, man.'

'Yes, sir,' de Brives de Moustier said miserably. 'I'll do what I can. *Ah, les salauds!*'

The Chairman had already banged the receiver down. 'That man is an imbecile,' he said to his empty office.

In Tokyo matters were ordered differently and with altogether less heat.

'It is with regret and apologies that I am talking to you,' Mr Sanjiro Konoda said on the telephone from his hotel bedroom to one of his board colleagues, and proceeded to tell him what had occurred. He too had heard that it was the work of the British.

'What are your wishes now, Konoda-san?' the colleague asked.

They talked at some length, Mr Konoda turning for advice from time to time to his three junior colleagues sitting in a neat row on his bed. Decisions were taken and polite farewells exchanged.

Over at the Hilton, the American contingent of three, led by one Harold B. Svensen, was in almost continual telephone communication with their head office in Fort Worth, Texas.

'What I want to know, Harold,' the President of Galactic Oil Industries said, 'is why it takes a British outfit to organize this kind of circus in *our* country. Aren't we capable, Harold, of getting a show like this on the road?'

'I guess we are, Sam.'

'So why didn't we do it, Harold? That's all I'm asking – why we didn't do it.'

'We had other things lined up.'

'All right. This is an open line. I don't want it set to music, Harold. Not unless you want to sing it to a Senate Sub-Committee.'

'Well, you were asking so I was telling you.'

'Harold,' the President said. 'I am not going to accept what has happened. Can you hear me?'

'I hear you, Sam.'

'You heard what I said? I am just not going to eat crow like this. In our own backyard, Harold, for Godsakes, and a bunch of fucking Britishers too. So I'll tell you what I want you to do, Harold, and listen carefully because it's pretty damn plain to me that you don't know how to do the job we hired you for, and we'll talk about that later. But what I want you to do now, Harold, is get your ass over here right away – on the next fucking aeroplane. And remember, Fort Worth is in the USA and not in dear old England. Can you remember that, Harold?'

'Sure, Sam, sure. I'll get the next plane out.'

'And leave Bill Watts and Arnold whatsisname there, with Bill in charge'.

'Sure,' said the unhappy Harold. He wanted to explain matters but thought better of it.

'By the way,' the President said, 'which university is it?'

It was the question Harold Svensen had feared most. 'I don't know, Sam,' he said.

'Did you say you don't know?'

'That's right, Sam.'

'You mean to tell me all this has happened under your nose there in Jakarta and you don't *know*?'

'That's right, Sam. I guess it came as a surprise to us all.'

There was a long silence. At last the President brought himself to speak. His extreme distress was tangible half way round the world. 'Then find out, Harold,' he said slowly. 'Before you catch that plane, right?' There was infinite menace in his voice.

'Right Sam, will do.'

'And Harold.'

'Yes, Sam.'

'Your stock option, Harold.'

'Yes, Sam.'

'I'm withdrawing it, Harold, under clause 14a of your contract – misdemeanours, dereliction of duty and actions inimical to the interests and purposes of the corporation.'

A distant click told Harold Svensen that the conversation had come to an end.

He turned to Bill Watts and Arnold Foreman who were waiting anxiously in the room. 'I'm heading back to Fort Worth,' he said. 'Sam wants you to stay on. You, Bill, will be in command. And we have to get the name of the university. How the hell do we do that?'

They pondered. 'Could try impersonating the media,' Arnold said. He was a black from Tennessee and he was on the trip because the President of Galactic prided himself on his advanced views on the race question. He not only employed rather more than the usual quota of company blacks: he also insisted that every overseas delegation from the company should include a token ethnic – usually black or Hispanic. Lately several Vietnamese had been under intensive training for this purpose. 'I give these shitheads damn good jobs,' the President was heard to say. 'No one is going to call *me* a racist pig.'

'Try that, will you?' Harold Svensen said.

Arnold Foreman picked up the phone and asked for Entakan. He got through to the General's office. 'This is CBS News,' he said. 'Please tell me which US university is making an award to your General Nasturtion.' There was a long pause and voices could be heard in dispute. Then they told him.

Harold Svensen went down to the lobby of the hotel and put the information on fax for his President. Then he went over to the Pan Am office to talk about flights.

On the telephone to Hackberry later that day, Papadopoulos dictated to Suzie the exact terms in which the invitation was to be extended to the General. He also discussed a number of details with President Zimmermann including the scope and nature of the ceremony and the steps to be taken to arouse the interest of the media.

'It's strictly nothingsville,' the President said. 'Why would any newspaper editor in his right mind be interested in this character down from the trees parading around our campus in a cap and gown? They'd give more space to a failed mugging in downtown Phoenix.'

'We have to get coverage,' Papadopoulos said. 'Those are my instructions and we'll talk again when I've had a chance to think of something. Maybe I'll use one of the New York PR outfits.'

'I don't like too much exposure, you know.' The President sounded nervous.

'Don't worry. Leave it to me,' Papadopoulos said reassuringly.

Back in Jakarta, others were active. Hildegarde let it be known via Dr Sombolon that she had more information for Mr Pidduck. An assignation was therefore arranged for that night. Mr Sombolon was busy fixing various details with General Nasturtion's secretary. He also telephoned his cousin at the Ministry of Mines.

'The bids may now be found,' he said.

'Could we not extend matters?' his cousin asked. 'Perhaps further payments would be forthcoming.'

'I am sorry,' Mr Sombolon said. 'There is no possibility.'

'A pity,' his cousin said. 'It was not difficult at all.'

'I will see you next week about my share,' Mr Sombolon told him. They bade each other good night.

Later, the ill-constructed bed collapsed beneath the pounding it was receiving from Pidduck and Hildegarde and they transferred their naked and perspiring bodies to the second bed in the room. Hildegarde had faithfully reported the General's remarks, filtering out the interjections relating to his irrigation. George Pidduck had appeared grateful, if somewhat alarmed, at what she had to tell him, but she paid little attention. For she now felt within herself a sluggish but mounting surge of passion, which she mistook for love, for this wonderful man who could rouse and satisfy her so splendidly. She had not known such feelings within herself since spending three incredible days of almost constant fornication with a Senegalese ship's cook in Hamburg some years before. It had given her a taste for black men which she had not since been able to

85

gratify. This white man, however, was quite as satisfactory. And so her instinct, primeval in its utter simplicity, was to give pleasure in return. In the course of pursuing this objective according to her dim and uncertain lights, she had reduced him in the space of three hours to total, aching exhaustion. So weakened was he by her repeated onslaughts that he had lost the strength to resist them. It was an alarming vicious circle of which she was blissfully unaware.

'*Ich liebe dich,*' she growled heavily into his ear. '*Ich liebe dich, mein Putzi.* Once more you come, no?'

'*No,*' he moaned. 'For God's sake, woman, leave me alone. My back's giving me hell.'

'Love is best for bad back,' she cried, concentrating on his bedraggled member with terrifying singleness of purpose.

'Leave it alone,' he moaned. 'Christ, you're bloody insatiable!'

'What is that, insatiable?' she asked, looking up for a moment from her task.

'Never mind, just leave me alone, damn you.' But George Pidduck's sexual equipment appeared to be unaware of the exhaustion felt by the rest of his body and was responding, to his growing horror, to Hildegarde's ministrations.

'You bitch,' he cried, 'leave me alone, damn you.'

'Mmmmmm,' Hildegarde said, unwilling to abandon what she was doing. And once again she reflected that she had found the world's most satisfactory and virile lover. Also, he would be giving her fifteen hundred dollars for the information she had brought him. God was undoubtedly good to those who believed in Him.

Later, as she waited for Mr Sombolon in the hotel lobby, she caught sight of a beautiful black man at the desk. He looked round and caught her eye and she smiled at him. Arnold Foreman, who was waiting for a friend, smiled back. Then Mr Sombolon appeared and she accompanied him to the street.

CHAPTER
8

It has often been remarked that the only significant characteristic of military engagements is their utter confusion and unpredictability. This is because the ends willed by the protagonists tend, naturally enough, to be mutually exclusive and to provoke responses in the other party which can never be accurately predicted or suitably catered for. If only Napoleon had let Wellington and Blucher get on with winning the battle of Waterloo there wouldn't have been all that mayhem of torn-off limbs, eviscerated horses and burning farmhouses. Indeed, Blucher wouldn't have been needed at all and it would have been in truth the great British victory (though won by an Irishman) that the history books want it to be. But the great battles of history, far from being affairs of orderly move and countermove, were nothing so much as a series of shambles dominated by blind chance, in which more or less incompetent leaders, invariably misinformed and ill-advised, tried unsuccessfully to keep up with events and, possibly, to influence them.

It is not too fanciful to liken the events of the present chronicle to some such military campaign. For the vectors of forces generated by the various organizations and individuals involved were creating unforeseen and unpredictable situations. It was not surprising to find, of course, that several people fondly imagined that they were in control of these events. At one stage Bernard de Brives de Moustier had so believed together with his board in Paris. Alas for them – a chimera! Mr Sombolon, after his interview with General Nasturtion, inherited this illusion, which he now shared with George Pidduck, though being subtler and more cynical than the Frenchman he realized that no commitments existed truly until a contract bore all the required signatures, and even then there were escape hatches for those who knew where to look for them. General Nasturtion, a man of frightening self-confidence and enormous ego, believed that he and he alone was in control and could impose his will on everyone else.

Needless to say, they were all wrong.

Immediately following the interview and their conversation, Mr Sombolon's cousin at the Ministry of Mines removed the bids from his private safe and opened them. Entakan's specifications, drawn up under General Nasturtion's precise instructions, had been so vague in a number of carefully chosen essentials that the bids could not be logically compared. It was a clear case of apples and pears, which is what the General needed in order to be able to choose a particular bid regardless of price. Any expert and unbiased examination of these tenders would have revealed the Japanese submission as the cheapest, even after the anomalies had been ironed out. This was because it contained a hidden and internationally banned subsidy from the Japanese Government – the only body politic in the world to know a thing or two about exporting and to act on the knowledge. They had put a few hundred million yen of taxpayers' money into the deal. Also, the Japanese bid carried the best delivery dates and service conditions. Faced with all this, and after a confidential discussion with the Minister, the General rejected it on the grounds that the hydraulic pumps and certain other items did not conform to specifications (no one's pumps did: the spec had been so written as to secure such an outcome).

The French price was the highest, which was now used to eliminate them, and the American offer was rejected unread on the grounds that it was not drawn up in due form and had in any case been received twenty-four hours after the closing date – neither of which contentions was true. It was therefore announced by Entakan that subject to certain assurances and the drafting of suitable documents, the contract for the coming year would be awarded to All World Oil Services of London and was worth a little in excess of 16.4 million dollars US. But this news did not deter the losers for one moment, for until a contract had actually been signed . . .

'This is not like other years,' Mr Sombolon said to his brother. 'I am not at ease with this arrangement and I am not sure why.'

'It would be safer with a simple gift of money,' the doctor said wisely.

'You are right. For instance, it seems to me dangerous to take the General to the United States. England would have been safer. It is a pity that the famous University at Oxford cannot do this thing. Also, I cannot forget the General's latest remarks to the German woman. We are walking on soft sand.'

'Will you go to America with them?'

'Certainly. It is an opportunity to strengthen my relationship with the General.'

'I read in the newspapers,' Doctor Sombolon said, 'that there are financial difficulties at Entakan. It is said they may default this month on the interest payments on their foreign borrowings. Is this serious?'

His brother waved away such peccadilloes. 'I too have read about it,' he said. 'The interest amounts to 100 million dollars per month – 1.2 billions annually just to service their overseas borrowings. If it were less it would be disastrous for them to default, but with such an enormous commitment the foreign banks will not dare to press too hard for fear of bankrupting them, in which case they would get none of their money back. No, our Government will have to help them out and I've no doubt the banks are already in touch with the Ministry of Finance.'

'Can this affect your deal?'

'Impossible. Without a servicing contract they can't operate the wells.'

Next morning at the hotel Mr Sombolon was talking to Pidduck in the lobby when the four Japanese came down in the lift with their bags. They bowed to Pidduck and Mr Sombolon. Mr Konoda smiled toothily and advanced. 'We must congratulate,' he said. 'Very fine achievement by your famous company. We wish much success for contract.' All four of them bowed again.

'Thank you,' Pidduck said, 'that's very decent of you, I'm sure. You leaving?'

'We go Tokyo now. All finished here. No success for us, but perhaps next time.' They shook hands and followed their luggage out into the rain.

'Not good people,' Mr Sombolon said. 'Damn Japs not sincere. Konoda not a gentleman.'

'He doesn't look it, either,' Pidduck agreed. 'It's a bit of a relief to see the back of them.'

At the far end of the lobby Bernard de Brives de Moustier sat in deep debate with a compatriot, his bird-like face bobbing about, his entire head of hair seeming to bristle with indignation.

'Other man is from damn French Embassy,' Mr Sombolon said. 'I think after my informations to the General about Legion of Honour it will be many years before Entakan gives contracts to damn French. Ho, ho, yes.'

A day or two later, on the far side of the globe, President Harvey Zimmerman of the University of Southern Arizona had a visitor. 'I'll try it, Harold,' he was saying. 'It's a difficult offer to refuse, so I'll try it.'

'That's great, Harvey,' Harold Svensen said.

'I'd sooner do business even with a Texan than a fucking limey,' the President said. 'All I have to do now is tell 'em to get lost.'

'Will that be difficult?'

'Hell, no. I'll just call the fat Greek and tell him to forget it. Tell you what, Harold, we'll do that right now. Just watch me.' He looked up a number in a desk directory and punched it out on the phone. A moment later he asked for Nicos Papadopoulos.

'Hi, there, Nicos,' he said, pumping joviality into his voice, 'this is Harvey Zimmerman. How've you been?'

'Great, Harvey, just great,' Papadopoulos said. 'What can I do for you?'

'It's just this, Nicos,' the President replied. 'I have to tell you that at this time I guess our deal is off. I can't do it, Nicos, and I sure am sorry to disappoint a great guy like you, but . . .'

'What the hell are you talking about?' Papadopoulos demanded. He sensed that this man would ride all over him if he failed to establish the upper hand. 'What's this crap about the deal being off?' It *can't* be off. It's too damn late to be off. So stop talking rubbish, will you?'

'I'm not doing that, Nicos,' Zimmerman said, careful not to let Svensen know he was being verbally assaulted in this fashion. 'Fact is, we've had a rival offer in the same field and it's far better than yours. No percentage there, you know. No pussycats. Unfortunately it comes to us in such a form we have to choose: we can't take both.'

'Who is it from?'

'I'm not at liberty to say, Nicos.'

'Well, whoever it is, you'll turn it down and like it.'

'Sorry, Nicos, I can't do that. There's another hundred grand involved and I'm a businessman.'

'You're a goddamn shyster.'

'Not that, Nicos,' Zimmerman said, forcing a laugh. 'I know you don't mean that, feller.'

'Don't I, by Christ?' Papadopoulos yelled into the mouthpiece. 'Don't I, you two-timing drygoods merchant! I'll tell you what, Zimmerman, and you listen to me carefully. You listening?'

'Yes, Nicos, I'm listening.' Zimmerman was sweating despite the arctic air-conditioning, and Harold Svensen could see the droplets of perspiration forming on his brow. The man at the other end must be pretty jumpy, he thought. Where had the President's abrasive tycoonery suddenly gone to? Harold Svensen fidgeted uneasily.

'So listen to this, Zimmerman,' Papadopoulos was saying. 'You go ahead with this new thing of yours and here's what I'll do. I'll get the IRS crawling all over your crummy University's books for a start. I take it you've got plenty to hide from Inland Revenue, so you'll simply love that. Then I'll lobby every last member of your Board of Regents and suggest they look into the circumstances in which Suzie stopped being an undergraduate and became whatever she became. I'll get them to take a look at the sleeping arrangements while I'm about it. Are you still listening, Zimmerman?'

'I'm with you, Nicos, I'm with you,' the President said. His handkerchief was out, mopping at his brow, and Harold Svensen noticed his hand wasn't steady.

'Now then, Zimmerman, I want you to understand me,' Papadopoulos continued. 'Those are just the first two things I'll do. There are others that it'll be my pleasure to reveal to you as we go along. You can guess what they are because you know best how vulnerable you are, right, Zimmerman?'

'Come on now, Nicos,' the President said, 'you don't need to take it so hard. It was only a suggestion, for Chrissakes. Give me a little rope, will ya?'

'A little rope, you said? Why, I'll *hang* you, Zimmerman, from one of your own wrought iron brackets, if I hear another word about calling the deal off.' Despite the distance between them, Papadopoulos sensed that he had his man on the run.

'Tell you what, Nicos,' the President said. 'I'll call you back, right? Let me get this little thing sorted out and I'll call you right back.'

'Make it within thirty minutes,' Papadopoulos said, 'and make it good. I haven't got all day.'

President Zimmerman turned to Harold Svensen. 'I'm sorry, Harold,' he said, 'but I guess I can't do it. This fucking Greek has pointed to certain difficulties – prior obligations and crap like that – which make it impossible. A pity – yours was a very fine scheme and it would have been a pleasure to do business with you. Maybe some other time.'

Back in Fort Worth later, Harold Svensen reported this failure to the President of Galactic. It was not a relaxed meeting.

'So you boobed again, Harold?' the President said. 'My, my, this is not your year, is it now?'

'The man said he couldn't unscramble his commitment, Sam,' Harold Svensen said.

'You mean you couldn't persuade him, Harold – not even with all those dollars in your fist you couldn't persuade him. You couldn't *sell* him, right?'

'I tell you, Sam, the guy was scared. They must have threatened him or something. I tell you, he's strictly off the wall. The whole place is weird. It's full of low-rent types, women without shoes, stuff like that. Why, he told me he's even got a hundred Japs there, paid for by some outfit back in Tokyo. And a couple dozen black guys in fezes from Zanzibar. Who ever heard of Zanzibar?'

The President of Galactic sighed like a man much put upon by fools. 'So what do we do now, Harold, tell me that?'

'Well, Sam,' Harold Svensen said unwisely, 'I guess we're licked on this one. Can't win 'em all.'

The President of Galactic had learned his business philosophy in a hard school. He had sold crude in the spot market to refiners who didn't need it and had chartered tankers from crooked Greeks, Japanese and Koreans. What he had retained from all this was a simple belief: you were never licked until the other guy had actually delivered and was being paid. In his day he'd seen contracts stolen, signatures falsified, bank officials suborned and deals overturned. He was wedded to the belief that red-blooded Americans, and more particularly Texans, never accepted defeat until they lay bleeding and senseless, as it were, in the dust.

'Harold,' he said quietly, 'you are making me throw up. You are making me throw up so much, you're fired. I'm taking over the Entakan thing myself and I'm not through with this shithouse in Arizona yet. Get Bill Watts back here from Jakarta right away, and I'll get the Controller to talk to you about your own contract and how we're to terminate it. We'll want your desk and your key to the men's room by five o'clock.' He got up and extended a large hand. 'I guess I'm sorry we never made out, Harold, but that's how the dice fall. Remember me to Mary. A lovely lady.'

There were a couple of weeks to go to the great day at Hackberry and during that time the President of Galactic thought long and hard. Midway through the week Bill Watts arrived from Jakarta and was immediately summoned to the President's office where he was offered Harold Svensen's Vice-presidency, a substantial hike in salary, Harold Svensen's key and a better make of car. Then, before he'd had time to recover from a nasty case of jet lag, he was ordered out to the campus at Hackberry. For the President had had an idea which he described to his wife as probably the finest piece of thinking in his career to date. 'As you know darn well,' he told her, 'we strive for excellence in the company. It's the name of the game. Well, this time I've achieved it.'

'Yeah?' his wife said. 'So what is this fantastic piece of thinking? Something Einstein missed there while he was doing his sums?'

'It's none of your damn business what it is,' her husband said, 'and don't sneer. It's thinking like that pays for your macramé classes.'

'Big deal,' she said.

Bill Watts's instructions were precise. They were also embedded in a simple threat: success at Hackberry and his Vice-presidency went together. One did not exist without the other. Before he went he called Arnold Foreman in Jakarta, and explained to him what the President of Galactic was now calling his game plan. 'Listen, Arnold,' he said, 'we need quotes – plenty of 'em. Stuff the General has said about the Americans and the Japs. Only the bad-mouthing, mind. You'd better

94

start digging. What time is it there?'

'Five am,' Arnold said, and yawned.

'Right. Put whatever you can on fax by eleven your time. I don't know how you'll do it but Sam says it has to be done.'

'Yeah,' Arnold said. 'I'll do what I can.'

'And keep it flowing. I'll be out on the campus, God help me, but I'll be calling the office here and they'll feed it to me as it comes in.'

'Right.'

'And add in anything else you come across which could make a Jap sore.'

'If you say so.'

Also midway through the week Nicos Papadopoulos flew out to Arizona and was again picked up by Suzie in her Buick at the airport at Flagstaff.

'Hi, there, Mr Papadopoulos,' she said and leant over his stomach and kissed him on the cheek. She smelt of jasmine.

'Hi, Suzie,' Papadopoulos said. 'What's new in Hackberry?'

'Well, we have every little thing lined up for the big day,' she told him. 'There'll be a great turnout and President Zimmerman has told the faculty members what he'll do to them if they don't all appear at the ceremony. He's very, very firm with the faculty. I think that's great.' She was taking the big car down hills and round sharp bends. 'I simply love big shows like this. Don't you just? With a band and all that stuff.'

'Yes, I do, Suzie,' Papadopoulos lied.

'You-all know we had that gentleman here from that company down in Fort Worth who wanted us to take their grant in place of yours.'

'I certainly do. Has he been around again?'

'No, sir. Why, President Zimmerman told him he was committed to you. That's what he said: committed. And President Zimmerman is a truly straight person, you know. A person who'd never break his word.'

'Sure,' Papadopoulos said. The woman was besotted

with the little bastard. Extraordinary!

Later he spent an hour with Suzie and President Zimmerman checking the details of the guests' accommodation, their dietary requirements, the ceremony itself, the logistics and coverage by the media. This last aspect still made the President visibly nervous, but he was now afraid of provoking another outburst from Papadopoulos and so said nothing. He knew when he was out of his league. With everything settled to his satisfaction, Papadopoulos was driven back to Flagstaff by Suzie to catch his flight to Phoenix and on to New York. From there he was to fly later to Los Angeles to await the arrival of the Nasturtion party from Jakarta and then escort them on to Hackberry. He could think of a dozen things he would sooner be doing.

Arnold Foreman might be the token black in the Galactic team but he was far from being simple. Indeed, it was the token system itself which was preventing him from being included in foreign negotiations on his own merits: he could be there as a black but he couldn't be there as anything else. Shortly after eight he was in the Public Relations department of Entakan. He told them he wanted to read through General Nasturtion's speeches of the past few years. The young Indonesian in charge looked at him as if he were mad. 'General Nasturtion makes many speeches,' he said. 'The files are very big.' He waved towards a long shelf full of box files.

'That's all right. Show me what you have in English and I'll read the stuff.'

The young man shrugged and showed Arnold Foreman to a chair and table and began feeding him files. After a couple of hours Arnold had several sheets of notes. 'This will be fine for now,' he said. 'I'll be back for more later.'

'Very good,' the young man said. He had never before encountered such interest in what the General had to say.

Arnold made his way out to the lobby. At the desk

stood a generously built blonde. He had noticed her before in the lobby of the Hotel Surabaya. As he approached the desk to surrender his security chit, she turned and saw him and again gave him a slow but generous smile. Hildegarde had remembered him from their first encounter. She had also remembered her Senegalese ship's cook from Hamburg and had got the two images confused in her mind. And since she recalled her Senegalese lover with affection it seemed natural to her to smile at this other black man who put her so strongly in mind of him.

'Hi,' Arnold said.

'Good day.' She smiled, showing her fine teeth.

'Saw you the other day.'

'*Ja.* From Hotel Surabaya going out.'

'Right. You work here?'

'No, no. I just visit friend.'

'Where you from?'

'I am German girl. You are Senegalese, yes?'

'Hell, no. American.'

They walked towards the door together. 'I'll buy you a drink,' Arnold said. 'Over there at the café.' He pointed to a place across the street.

'Now I cannot. I must go to my house. But other time is possible.' It was difficult, even dangerous, to get out, but Hildegarde had rediscovered her Senegalese – or what appeared to be a passable substitute for him – and she had a plan. A few days from now the General would be leaving for the United States. It would be easier to arrange a meeting.

'When can we meet, honey?' Arnold asked.

'Next Thursday, *ja*, I meet you in bar in Hotel Surabaya at half eight. Is good?'

'Is great.'

She blew him a girlish kiss and climbed into a taxi. The Englishman would be gone by then too. A girl needed consolation. It would have been lonely, but now she had found someone interesting. Anneliese would make one of her scenes. Why were women always so terribly jealous?

CHAPTER
9

The last few days in Jakarta before the departure of the General's caravan for the United States saw a good deal of activity, some in the blazing light of the popular media, some between consenting adults in private. The newspaper editors, experienced in the ways of army generals, had heeded the warning and placed General Nasturtion's announcement of the US trip on their front pages. They had contrived, at the expense of their professional standards, to keep the subject there ever since. They ran further interviews with the General, a statement from George Pidduck, an interview with the General's wife which had been run up by an Entakan PR man, and details about the University of Southern Arizona supplied for a fee by Mr Sombolon from his capacious imagination.

The General was seen again on television, answering questions all of which he had devised himself. Desperate for relief from the unctuous tedium of the encounter, the interviewer had slipped in a question of his own about Entakan's financial situation and had been dismissed for his pains the following day.

But the newspapers were picking up stories from the *Wall Street Journal* and the *Financial Times*. These reported a meeting in New York of representatives of the lead banks in the consortium which had lent Entakan several billion dollars and who were now screaming discreetly, as only bankers can, for their interest. Any idea of capital repayments now appeared so remote as to be laughable, and the representative of an Italian bank who suggested it at the meeting was in fact greeted with a round of sardonic laughter from the dozen or so assembled bankers. It was not an attractive sound. A day of animated discussion produced, with great travail, an agreed decision: they would meet again. Meanwhile they would observe solidarity and enter into no unilateral deals, no moratorium and no refinancing except by mutual agreement. The Germans, who after the Americans had most money at stake, opposed the resolution. They wanted tougher action. But having lost, they agreed to abide by its terms. The Japanese, from the Imperial Bank of Tokyo, also in it up to their ears, said nothing at all.

'Equivocating little yellow bastards,' the representative of the UK banks remarked to his French colleague over a gin and tonic after the meeting. 'They're up to no good. I don't like their silence.'

'Their situation is different,' the Frenchman said. 'The Indonesians are more dependent on Japanese trade, including their purchases of Entakan oil. Also, the Imperial Bank of Tokyo has big interests in the trading companies who do the business with Indonesia. It's difficult for the Japanese to stay with us on this.'

'What do you think they'll do?'

'I have no idea, but you have to consider that their trading relationship gives them more influence in Jakarta than we can have. In Indonesian eyes our countries are scarcely more than moneylenders, whereas Japan is a most important customer as well. The Japanese are bound to try to exploit that special position.'

'Anyway,' the Englishman said, 'I've no time for the Nips. None at all. Never have had.'

'Please, Nips?'

'Nips – Nipponese – Japs – little yellow bastards – it's all the same.'

'Oh, I see.'

The Jakarta newspapers failed to capture the flavour of all this. They merely ran the story of the meeting and its communiqué, and under official pressure they wrote accompanying editorials of extreme virulence attacking Western financial institutions for their hard-nosed greed. General Nasturtion was quoted as saying all commitments would be honoured. He didn't say when or by whom.

So much for official events, more or less publicly reported. In the General's eyes, however, the big event of the week was the arrival of the German ladies. There proved to be only two of them: Waldtraute and Sieglinde Borkh. The third girl, who was very short-sighted and vague in her manner, had wandered off in Bangkok and had not been seen since. But Waldtraute and Sieglinde were truly magnificent – if pink-and-white bulk, topped with pale yellow tresses, all in duplicate, was one's feminine ideal. The resident Germans had been warned of their arrival and had accepted the inevitable with more or less good grace, though Anneliese had foretold gloomily that the General was now likely to discard a few of the present incumbents in favour of the newcomers. She didn't see how such a busy man could cope with the enlarged staff. His colon, in her view, would never stand it.

The twins proved to be amiable in a heavy North German kind of way, given to hearty and even deafening laughter when, at last, they saw the point of a joke, always with Waldtraute a little ahead of Sieglinde. For though neither of them was brainy, Sieglinde could be described as less brainy than Waldtraute, thus finding herself in one of the IQ bands that the educationists regularly despair of. Perhaps it was this lack of intellectual sparkle that led them almost at once to strike up a friendly relationship with Hildegarde, to the distress of the pathologically jealous Anneliese. For Hildegarde's part, it was refreshing to the spirit to hear gossip from the homeland, to giggle over an exchange of curiously similar sexual experiences, and to borrow from the twins' stock of romantic magazines and paperbacks. She tried on their clothes, swapped a couple of T-shirts, and amid gasps and enormous guffaws of laughter explained in precise anatomical and technical detail what the General would expect of them in the way of services.

'I heard of this,' Waldtraute said, 'but I have never done it.'

'No,' Sieglinde said, 'mostly we did group sex or dressing up crazy, you know. A little S/M too, but I hate to be hurt.'

'Me too,' Hildegarde said. 'But this irrigation thing is easy. Disgusting, of course, and very boring, but no trouble at all. And you just do it once and that's all till the next time. He likes to go to bed early. Not like those insatiable brutes who are at you all night.'

'Good,' Waldtraute said. 'We like to sleep a lot.'

'And we like a little time for our own fun together,' Sieglinde said, 'don't we?'

Waldtraute nodded and gave her sister a playful slap.

'The men like the fact that you're twins?' Hildegarde asked.

They nodded vigorously. 'Some of them pay big money, the perverted swine.' They rumbled and gasped with laughter.

'I don't see,' Hildegarde said, 'how the General can use both of you for his high colonics. It only needs one person. Unless he wants you to take it in turns, but that would be silly.' She was puzzled.

'Maybe one of us must do the waterworks while the other looks after him in front,' Waldtraute said.

'You'd think any normal man would want something like that,' Hildegarde said, 'but not this little twerp. He does that for himself. He won't let you touch it. It's too precious. And even if . . .' The end of her remark was lost in another wave of guttural laughter.

'You can never tell what men will want,' Sieglinde gasped. 'Why, once in Mannheim we were with an old boy who just wanted us to stroke his bum with a lot of twigs. He was a multi-millionaire, too. Just twigs, it was, from the park. It was his private park. I suppose he kept it for the twigs. In Mannheim, that was, a lousy hole, wasn't it? But we saw *The Sound of Music* there. That was lovely.'

Waldetraute nodded. 'Sieglinde only likes Dusseldorf,' she said. 'She likes the shops there, don't you, Linde?'

Sieglinde agreed. 'They have all the best movies in Dusseldorf, too. And the cake shops are good.'

They rambled on about the strange tastes of men and the rival attractions of German cities. It was the kind of undemanding conversation that Hildegarde enjoyed. It didn't put a strain on her mind.

Later they fitted out the Borkh twins with boots, helmets, cloaks and a couple of shields, and integrated them in one of their tableaux in time for the General's evening visit. He watched their dreary and talentless miming with warm approval and clapped when the other girls mounted a mock attack with their spears, forcing the twins to manipulate their inadequate shields with a good deal of speed amid grunts, shouts and squeals of alarm.

'Oh, oh, excellent!' cried the General. 'They are extraordinary – absolutely identical and so blonde. What splendid white bottoms they have! *Four* cheeks between them,' and he laughed uproariously at his remark. The sight of all this milky flesh and the thought of the delights to come were making the General tumescent. He was impatient to be alone with the twins. 'Did you instruct them?' he asked Hildegarde.

'*Ja, mein Nasty.*'

'Do they understand? Will they do all that is needed?'

'Sure, why not, if you give them nice present?'

'Do they know how to work the apparatus – the correct temperature for the water and so on?'

'*Ja, ja.*'

'Good. I think I will go to their room now. I have had enough of this nonsense.'

Hildegarde, ever generous, gave the twins a piece of parting advice. 'Push hard on the nozzle,' she said, 'Don't worry about hurting him. The more you damage him the more he'll give you. He's crazy. And all that water, too.'

The following morning at eight the General called in Mr Sombolon for a final briefing. He was in high good humour – something exceedingly rare in the office. 'Ha,' he said by way of greeting, 'your German twins, Sombolon. Magnificent! A great experience!'

Mr Sombolon inclined his head. 'Thank you, General. As you know, I humbly do my best.'

'Well, this time your best is outstanding and I give you full marks. It's what I want to talk to you about.'

'Yes, General?'

The General fixed him with a dominating stare. 'I want those girls to come to America with us and I want you to make the necessary arrangements. Understand, my wife and children are with me, so the girls must travel separately. It must all be very discreet. You will fix transport, their accommodation at the University – everything. The accommodation must be convenient.'

Mr Sombolon thought he saw a snag which would kill the whole appalling idea. 'And their visas?' he asked.

'No problem,' the General said. 'I am getting our Ministry of Foreign Affairs to approach the US Embassy here. It will be done in forty-eight hours as a favour to my wife.'

'To your wife?'

'Yes, they travel as her hairdresser and masseuse, though she will not know of this arrangement, of course. It is purely administrative. If anything, they are my masseuses.' He laughed and Mr Sombolon obligingly did the same. 'So is that understood, Sombolon?'

'Certainly, General,' Mr Sombolon said. He was disturbed. As if the whole thing were not complicated and dangerous enough without having two fat German sibling tarts with dubious visas mixed into it. Mr Pidduck would not be pleased, at the cost or the complications. And he, Sombolon, would have a lot more legwork for which he could as yet see no return.

Though that was not strictly true. His fertile mind, searching for points at which money might change hands, was already homing in on a number of possibili-

ties. 'May I make a humble suggestion, General?' he
said.

'What is it, Sombolon?'

'These twins – they are very fine girls, high-class,
sincere and affectionate. But you know women – they
are all talkative, greedy and ultimately treacherous. I
think you should not tell them they are to go to the
United States until the very last moment. They may talk
and some malicious person may warn the US Embassy.
And that would be bad because the Americans have
strict laws on what they call moral turpitude.'

'Oh, yes, Sombolon?'

'Indeed. If you have a mad grandmother it is not
possible for you to emigrate to the United States. Also
if you have ever been in jail, even overnight and as a
regrettable mistake by the police. Also if you have been
a member of the Communist Party. Also if you have
been a whore.'

'But these girls of yours aren't Communists?'

'Certainly not.'

'Have they been in jail?'

'Never.'

'Is there lunacy in their family?'

'Not that I know of.'

'So?'

'In the eyes of the Americans,' Mr Sombolon said,
averting his gaze, 'they could be classified as whores.
The Americans are very narrow minded.'

'That is idiotic,' the General said. 'You told me they
came from very distinguished families.'

'They do, from the highest class of German society.
But try telling that to the American Immigration
Service if they have heard malicious rumours to the
contrary.'

'Very well, I will keep it a secret until the eve of our
departure. Your advice is good.'

'Your decisions, as always, are exceedingly wise,' Mr
Sombolon said.

The General then moved on to other matters. 'Are all

the preparations made?' he asked.

'Yes, General, all.'

'While we are in Los Angeles the children will want to visit the movie studios and Disneyland.'

'No problem.'

'My wife will go shopping.'

Mr Sombolon inclined his head. He could not bring himself to say 'No problem' when he thought of the bills that rapacious woman would run up.

'And don't forget, at the University the twins must be in convenient accommodation – convenient for me to visit them.'

'Certainly.'

'In Los Angeles put them in a nearby hotel.'

'I have already made a note to that effect,' Mr Sombolon said.

'Such buttocks,' the General said, half to himself. 'I never saw such splendid buttocks.'

Dr Sombolon had been quick to add the delectable twins to his panel of patients. 'Prophylaxis is very important for girls in your position,' he told them.

'Ah,' Sieglinde said. She did not know what it meant but she stood in awe of doctors.

'You are fortunate in that I look after all the girls here. I will be happy to give you both a fortnightly examination and any treatment you may need. Of course, the General will pay.'

'*Zehr gutt!*' Waldtraute said.

'I will give you your first examinations now,' the Doctor said, his eyes betraying signs of unprofessional excitement. Hildegarde translated for him and added a remark of her own which led to an ill-suppressed guffaw. The Doctor had a joyful time going over the two big, pink bodies in intimate detail. He found no lumps when palpating their breasts but went over them twice to make sure. 'Perhaps I shall prescribe a little ointment,' he said. 'It is always good as a precaution in the genital region, which can become overheated in our climate and thus vulnerable to infection. I will bring some next time and show you both how to apply it in order to maintain your genito-urinary tracts in a clean and healthy condition.'

'There you are, what did I tell you?' Hildegarde said in German. 'The dirty swine will poke his fingers in, you see.'

'Also,' Dr Sombolon went on, 'I would like you, Miss Glauber, to translate into German for me the following message from my brother. He says that by a fortunate chance he is in a position to influence General Nasturtion to take the Borkh sisters with him to the United States. Also, my brother has influence at the American Embassy and can obtain visas for them. He asks whether they would be interested.'

Hildegarde translated. The answer, amid squeals of delight, was affirmative.

'Good,' Dr Sombolon said, 'and please tell them that unfortunately there will be some costs attached to the plan. The General intends to give them both some money. Out of this my brother will have to give gifts at the embassy. Getting visas is a very difficult and delicate business.'

Hildegarde translated again.

'The sum will be five hundred dollars each, which they can pay to my brother later. Meanwhile, absolute secrecy is essential. The General will no doubt want it to be a surprise and will claim it was all his own idea. They must naturally pretend to believe this.'

All this produced a high state of excitement and assurances of absolute discretion. Then Dr Sombolon left for home, lost in admiration for his brother's limitless ingenuity and well pleased with his new patients.

The day before the departure from Jakarta the official contract reached George Pidduck. After reading it through three times and marking some dubious passages he called Pipe in London. 'I've got the contract here,' he said. 'It doesn't look bad – more or less follows the detail of our tender.'

'What are the penalty clauses like?'

'Just the usual.'

'Anything fishy?

'Not really. If we had time I'd query a few points, but my advice is to sign and argue later if we have to. It's still touch-and-go here.'

'Where's the danger coming from?'

'Who knows with this chap? At any rate, I think the frogs are scuppered.'

'Good show.'

'It won't be cheap, mind you.'

'I don't want to know,' Pipe said hastily.

'Didn't think you would,' Pidduck said.

Then Daphne took the call back. 'How are you, my lovely?' Pidduck asked her.

'I'm fine. I miss you. When's Rome, then?'

He told her about the US trip. 'Oh, shit,' she said.

'Never mind,' he said. 'One of these days I'll take you to Clacton.'

When Mr Sombolon took the signed contract back to Entakan headquarters he was told that the General had departed for the day and would not be back in his office until after his American visit. Mr Sombolon realized that the timing had been very precisely engineered: there was to be no signature until the General had his cap, his gown, his certificate and his picture in the *New York Times*. That and all the stuff his wife would buy at Bergdorf Goodman and Gucci. It was pointless to argue; so Mr Sombolon, ever mindful of his personal standing with Entakan, did not argue.

That night, two things happened in Jakarta that merit brief comment. The first was that Arnold Foreman of Galactic filed his last fax of quotes from General Nasturtion's speeches. It contained a reference to 'monstrous Japanese hegemony' and 'the unbridled and uncontrolled bolshevik activities of the Japanese student body'. Arnold thought that might come in useful. The second was that in a farewell burst of furious coupling, George Pidduck and Hildegarde Glauber broke the second bed.

CHAPTER
10

The departure from Jakarta airport of the Nasturtion party passed off without incident. The press and TV corps were there *en masse*, fearful of the consequences of staying away. Pictures were taken and interviews given. Mr Sombolon took a group of newspapermen aside and told them that never before had an American university awarded an honorary Ph.D. to a foreigner. 'And even if they have,' he added confusingly, 'it was not to a personality from the Third World. And even in the Third World, never to an Indonesian.' He also remarked that discussions were under way with the White House for the General to be received in the Oval Office if he chanced to get down as far as Washington. 'I had the honour of organizing all this,' he said. 'You may mention that fact in your newspapers.' He then offered to cover the proceedings for anyone who might be interested. There were no takers: ever sensitive to the needs of the media, the General had included four journalists in his party.

George Pidduck was glad to get out of Jakarta. It had been a nerve-racking assignment, and wet with it. He hoped never to have another like it. Now that the thing seemed set fair for success he should have felt better. But he decided that he didn't. An anxiety, almost a foreboding of mayhem to come, had seized him in the last few days and wouldn't let go. The American venture had been his idea and he was proud of it. It had been a last throw in a losing situation and so far it had paid off. But he didn't feel at ease about it. He was spending very large sums of company money and the General hadn't actually signed anything. He hoped devoutly that Nicos had found the right university, that it wasn't some wretched backwoods dump where they didn't know how to lay on a decent show. He also hoped that none of the dozens of disasters which could occur on a jaunt like this would actually take place. He took his seat next to Mr Sombolon in the DC10 feeling restless and irritable. Mr Sombolon sensed it.

'Not greatest happiness is felt,' he said, 'though General now in our hands.'

'You're right,' Pidduck said.

'Greatest vigilance required,' Mr Sombolon said. 'Damn competitors do not lie down. Always they plot, isn't it. Only vigilance is good.'

Pidduck nodded and wondered what could go wrong in the coming week and who would make it so. Then he called for an extra cushion to put in the small of his back, which was troubling him, and tried to get some rest. Hildegarde had been a stimulating, even an extraordinary experience, but he felt a sense of relief as the plane widened the gap between them by an extra ten miles per minute. 'She'd have killed me,' he reflected as he closed his eyes. 'The woman was positively terrifying.'

For her part, Hildegarde was harbouring feelings of lust and longing which she wrongly identified as undying love for her wonderful Englishman. But the prospect of meeting the black stranger softened the blow and plunged her mind into a rather pleasing confusion of emotions. At the appointed time on the following day she was in the ill-lit hotel bar, sipping an orange squash and idly recalling the passionate days back in Hamburg with her Senegalese. Would this black man be like that one? Of course: weren't they both black? In her simplicity she believed all the clichés about nations and races. That was why she had been so astonished by the Englishman. For was it not true that those few Englishmen who were not homosexuals were of low potency and addicted to whips and other forms of correction? Yet this one was splendidly potent and hadn't as much as smacked her rump in jest.

When Arnold Foreman arrived they found each other in the gloom and chatted while Arnold drank a scotch. Then he took her over to the Hilton for dinner. Hildegarde put away great quantities of food, much of it potatoes, while Arnold watched in amazement. It took his mind off the dreadful inanity of her conversation, limited as it was by the thinness of her English vocabulary and still more by the emptiness of her mind. Between courses he searched for a subject which might evince something more than a beaming '*Jawohl*' from this slow-witted gastronomic freak. He had tried and failed to find out what she did. Between the steaks and the dessert he thought he might interest her in what he did.

'I'm here on business,' he said. 'For an American company.'

'Oil business?'

'Oil supplies. We're after a contract with Entakan. That's why I was there the other day. It's tough going, dealing with that guy Nasturtion.'

'*Jawohl!*' Hildegarde's mind was largely made up of recesses. Something stirred in the dimmest of them. Might this man be in the same business as her Englishman? Might they be after the same contract? Might they then be rivals? Her mind added supposition to supposition, slowly and with effort. It was all very confusing. She thought she might ask if he knew Mr Pidduck. But wouldn't that show that *she* knew him? Whereas, if she were very cunning perhaps she could get the black man to talk and once again she would have information with which to please her Englishman. It did not occur to her at that moment that she had no idea of how to convey that information to him, somewhere in the United States.

'My good friend is General Nasturtion,' she said. 'He told to me he will sign with British for contract.'

'Oh, no, he won't,' Arnold said with a touch of

flamboyance. 'Not when we've finished with him.'

'How you will do this?' Hildegarde asked, wide eyed.

'Maybe someone will balls up the initiation,' Arnold said.

'Balls *up*? Sorry, this I do not understand. I understand only balls.'

'Someone will play a few tricks out in Arizona. You know, spoil the party.'

'Please?'

'Forget it, honey,' Arnold said. 'Let's drink some cognac up in my room.'

Hildegarde made an effort to store in her mind what he had said, even though she didn't properly understand it. But playing tricks didn't sound good. Maybe she could get him to tell her some more later.

They drank their cognac and then she tested her theory that all black men, having blackness in common, must have sexual talent in common too. Afterwards, well pleased with the trial, she tried to get him to talk about the contract again, but all she could get out of him was a sleepy: 'You were great, honey. Why not stop talking so you can use your mouth for something else?' But though she had learned no more about the contract by the time she reached home, she had come to a firm conclusion: she must warn her Englishman of what the Americans were plotting against him. For was not playing tricks in Arizona some kind of plot? Having distilled this simple thought from the miasma of half-understood ideas in her mind, she now clung to it with dogged conviction. But how to reach the Englishman? Perhaps through Dr Sombolon.

Next day she called on him but there was no meeting of minds. Hildegarde held on to her scraps of information. She was not prepared to reveal them to intermediaries. For his part, having failed to get a word of what he regarded as sense out of the woman, Dr Sombolon decided he should not tell her how to communicate with his brother or George Pidduck. His offers to act as intermediary having been rejected, he came to the conclusion that Hildegarde probably knew nothing worth hearing and was up to some trick designed to extract money for nothing.

On her way home, Hildegarde slowly came to a decision: if she could reach the Englishman in no other way, she would go to him – over in Arizona – to warn him before it was too late. Yes, she would fly to the United States, save the contract and win his undying gratitude. She was not a highly imaginative girl, living as she did very much in the present moment or at most in the current week, but wonderful vistas seemed to her to open up: liberal supplies of money which she would carefully save, endless days and nights of lustful and deeply satisfying copulation, maybe marriage and a place in Court society as wife of this relative of the Queen of England! In this delightful fantasy she pictured herself in tiara and long white gloves, as she had seen them in the magazines, by the side of her Englishman in knee-breeches and buckled shoes. She curtseyed, and the Queen said a few gracious words and asked after her little ones, while her wonderful spouse looked proudly on. What might a girl not achieve with loyalty, a 50-inch bottom and a firm trust in God?

She redirected her taxi to a travel agency, wondering how one found one's way to Hackberry, Arizona, USA. For that was the only geographical indication she had, scribbled down without quite knowing why when the Englishman had mentioned it. Now she found the piece of paper in her handbag. She would make her way to Hackberry and the Englishman would be pleased with her . . .

Hildegarde in Jakarta struggled with the complexities of airline bookings and visa applications under conditions of strict secrecy, for Anneliese might throw an hysterical fit and the General's staff could prevent her leaving. General Nasturtion and his family and hangers-on in Los Angeles were meanwhile enjoying the amenities of the Beverly Hills Hotel, while the Borkh twins were equally at home not far away in the Beverly Wilshire. While the General's wife was cutting a swathe through the boutiques, the General was installed in bloated and exquisite discomfort on Waldtraute's bed, begging for more. Gratitude was a sentiment totally foreign to his gritty and unyielding nature, but he now became aware of feelings perilously close to gratitude: towards this fantastic pair and towards Mr Sombolon who had found them for him. All this must be rewarded, he reflected, as the girls continued to maltreat him and the great volume of water made its way along his intestinal tract. Then he lost sight utterly of these generous feelings as his oddly patterned psycho-sexual urges reached fulfilment.

With the General thus satisfied, his wife's store of Gucci impedimenta replenished and the Nasturtion children sated with Chocmint Ripple ice-cream and Mammothburgers, the time came to move on to Hackberry. With Papadopoulos in charge of logistics, they set out.

'So good, so far,' Mr Sombolon observed to George Pidduck as they settled into the plane for the flight to Phoenix.

'I know what you mean,' Pidduck said. 'It cost us a pretty penny in handbags and junk food in LA but I think it went well. The General spent a lot of time over at the Beverly Wilshire. He must be worn out.'

'He has much appreciations of the German sisters,' Mr Sombolon said with a touch of pride in his voice. 'My brother the doctor tells me they have very beautiful white bottoms. Also biggest knockers. This the General appreciates. Also they are very classy girls from highest German aristocracy. This gives the General much appreciation also. He does not like whores.'

Pidduck marvelled yet again at the heady mixture of the demotic and mandarin in Mr Sombolon's vocabulary. 'But how do you find these creatures?' he asked.

Mr Sombolon permitted himself a licentious wink and waggled his head gently from side to side in the style of

114

his friend from Madras. 'I know very fine agency in Germany run by lady of highest reputation. She supplies all types of girls all over world and for many purposes. An excellent lady for this type of business.'

'A German woman?'

'No, no, a very fine lady from a city in your country.'

'Which city might that be?'

'Runcorn.'

'My God!'

'Please?'

'I never thought of Runcorn as a home of international vice.'

'The girls,' Mr Sombolon continued, pleased to impart useful information, 'are from all countries of Europe.'

'Ah.'

'It is what I believe you call the European Economic Community, all currencies accepted and convertible, yes?'

'I never thought of the EEC quite like that either.'

'Girls,' Mr Sombolon said. 'Also boys. If you wish, I tell this lady your name and you get a very special price.'

'Ah, thanks, Mr Sombolon. I'll let you know.' And George Pidduck reflected that membership of the EMS had its mysteries and exotic byways like everything else.

'Boys not for you personally,' Mr Sombolon acknowledged, not wishing to offend, 'but sometimes this service is useful.'

Nicos Papadopoulos heaved his bulk out of his seat across the aisle and came over to them. 'I hope the media will be meeting us at Phoenix,' he said. 'Did you warn the General?'

Mr Sombolon nodded. 'I told him all great US newspapers and TV networks.'

'I never promised that,' Papadopoulos said in some alarm. 'It's far more likely to be the locals.'

'General will not know,' Mr Sombolon said simply. 'Belief that it is *New York Times* will cause much happiness for him.'

115

Nicos Papadopoulos had always operated on the 'no boomerang' principle: do not tell untruths which will return to smite you in the back of the neck later. He could not readily adjust to Mr Sombolon's eastern insouciance – the freer and altogether more imaginative lying born of a less materialistic culture. The distinction was fundamental and important. For Papadopoulos a lie was a reluctant alternative to the truth: reluctant because with a lie detection was always possible and with detection, problems. He lied when he had to, and always with the avoidance of detection in clear view.

For Mr Sombolon, a lie fulfilled a quite different function. It was a way of telling a man what that man wanted to hear, and thus of pleasing him and (as a hoped-for consequence) of earning respect, gratitude and obligation in his eyes – all of them recompensible states. He never worried about the likelihood of a lie being detected later, since the future was unpredictable anyway and opportunities would doubtless present themselves for dealing with whatever might befall. What man, after all, could truly foretell the eventual effect of what he said? What right had he to such presumption? Mr Sombolon, the modest pragmatist, had no such pretensions. And if General Nasturtion wanted the *New York Times* to be at the airport, was it not the merest kindness and courtesy to tell him the *New York Times* would be there? Indeed it was, and the act of so doing had nothing whatever to do with whether or not the *New York Times* would be there in reality. Also, was it not possible that the General could be persuaded that a reporter for the *Phoenix Times-Herald* was in fact the Chief of the West Coast Bureau of the *New York Times*?

A couple of rows ahead in the aircraft General Nasturtion sat with his wife, discussing how to fit in a further visit to Tiffanys, where she had seen a necklace of rubies and yellow diamonds which had been much to her taste.

CHAPTER
11

Bill Watts had been having a busy time on the campus on behalf of Galactic. He had picked up his first Japanese student in the local Howard Johnson and, presenting himself as a member of a human rights group in Dallas, had been passed on in a matter of hours to the leaders of the Japanese Students' Association. This body appeared to represent the 108 Japanese students in residence at the U of SA at Hackberry. The second meeting also took place in the Howard Johnson café. The young Japanese – two men and a girl – were polite and puzzled. Bill Watts once again presented his shaky credentials, which were received with 'Ah, so' and a certain amount of bowing from the waist. The Japanese spoke fair English. 'In what way can we be of assistance?' one of them asked.

'We in the civil rights movement,' Bill Watts said, 'are concerned about next week's ceremony – the award of a Ph.D. to this Indonesian General. D'you know about it?'

They nodded, wondering why he had come to them and not to one of the civil and human rights groups which flourished at U of SA. But they felt it would not be polite to enquire and so they said nothing.

'I'll be talking to other groups, of course,' Watts said, 'but we thought you would be specially interested because of General Nasturtion's violent anti-Japanese position. I suppose you know all about that.'

'Ah, so,' again.

Watts took some papers out of his pocket. 'Here,' he said, 'I have a bunch of quotes from Nasturtion's speeches and writings over the past five years. My, he certainly hates your guts.' He handed over the sheets, on which the choicest of the General's unwise remarks, ripped out of context and here and there firmed up a little, had been typed. The three students spent a few minutes swapping sheets and reading carefully.

'Also,' Watts pressed on, 'I have here our biographical notes on the General, showing his anti-left and anti-democratic role in the Indonesian army before he joined Entakan.' He handed over a further sheet. The students talked to each other in animated Japanese.

'This man appears to be a counter-revolutionary nationalist, possibly in the pay of Western imperialism,' the girl said. 'Please, why he is to receive Ph.D. at this University?'

'He's getting it because he paid for it,' Watts said. 'Or rather someone bought it for him. The whole thing's a phoney – an insult to academic standards, and of course to you Japanese.'

They conferred again. To Watts it sounded fairly heated. 'I have told my comrades,' the girl said, 'that running dogs of imperialism must be resisted by all democratic forces. This means Japanese students here at Hackberry must oppose award of Ph.D. by mass action. This can show will of democratic forces to overcome imperialism in all forms.'

'I guess that's right,' Watts agreed. 'I guess that's exactly what my group wants you to do – resist imperialism in all forms. What do you fellers say to that?'

'We wish to consider carefully in our committee,' one of the men said. 'We will look at all aspects of problem and take best decision for promoting unity of democratic forces.' The other man nodded.

'Please, what action your group proposes?' the girl asked.

'Well,' Watts said, 'we thought you and your friends could stage a demonstration during the ceremony. You know, a march with banners – something the media will pick up.'

They nodded. 'Your group wishes we smash reactionary plan for Ph.D?' the girl asked.

'That's about it,' Watts said. 'It would be great if this guy went away from here without it. D'you reckon you could do that?'

'We will consider in our committee,' the man said. 'If we agree such action desirable we will do all in our power to foil plans.'

There was more debate, the girl translating extracts from the papers on the table. She turned to Watts again. 'We discuss if action should be for Japanese students only or united front of all progressive organizations on campus. I believe united action best. My comrades not certain.'

'Hell, no,' Watts said hurriedly, trying to head off exactly what his President had warned him against. 'Don't you see, if we Americans demonstrate against General Nasturtion, the media will call it a racist plot – you know, Southern student body opposing award to distinguished Third World figure. Then he'll have all kinds of bleeding heart organizations backing him. But you are Asians, right, and no one could say your opposition was racist, right? So we reckon you Japanese should have all the action.'

This time the debate between them lasted ten minutes. 'We will consider this important aspect also,' one of the men said. 'We see value of your careful argument and beg you to let us reach good decisions.'

'Sure,' Watts said, 'you talk it over. But leave it to me to talk to the others. I'll tell 'em what your tactics are, so that you get support but no action from the Americans.' He had no intention of doing anything of the sort.

'International solidarity more important than stopping propaganda of fascist press,' the girl said firmly.

'I don't think that's right,' Watts said. 'My group is particularly hot on that point: no action from US organizations on campus – only the Japanese.'

'We will discuss your valuable suggestion and thank you sincerely for it,' the man said. 'Tonight we will

119

discuss. Respectfully suggest we meet again here tomorrow morning.' They fixed the details.

Bill Watts drove back to his hotel satisfied with the progress he had made. He called Fort Worth and dictated a report to the President's answering machine. Then he went down to the bar and did a lot of drinking to kill the rest of the day. Next morning, which was some forty-eight hours before the General was due to arrive, he was back in his regular booth at the Howard Johnson, drinking more coffee and eating his third doughnut. The Japanese students arrived precisely on time and joined him with small bows, smiles and handshakes. They ordered Cokes and the girl made a short speech.

'Last night our leading cadre considerd your interesting proposal, for which we thank on behalf of all Japanese students at Hackberry. We took clear decision this agent of imperialism must be taught lesson. We therefore accept your suggestion and will mobilize all Japanese students to oppose granting of Ph.D. Committee also accepts proposal that only Japanese shall demonstrate, thus breaking international solidarity. I must state left faction in committee, of which I am member, humbly disagrees but accepts majority decision.' She stopped and her two companions nodded.

'That's fine,' Watts said. 'Let's talk about the action you people can take.'

'Respectfully, this is question for planning committee set up at meeting last night. We request your utmost confidence. Our comrades will act in firm and disciplined way. Not possible to reveal action in advance.' Again the men nodded.

'Okay,' Watts said. 'I'm at the Holiday Inn if you need me. How can I contact you?'

They told him their names and how to find them on campus. Then they got up, repeated the ritual of their arrival, and departed. Watts went to the phone and called his President collect in Fort Worth.

'It's fixed,' he said.

'Japs only?' asked the President of Galactic.

'That's right.'

'Good work, Bill,' the President said. 'Now I want you to stay right in there and see that it happens, okay?'

'Yes, sir.'

'And see the others keep out of it, right?'

'Right.'

'How much did it cost?'

'Not a cent.'

'How did you swing it, then?'

'I did it all with ideology.'

'What the hell do you know about ideology?'

'I was at UCLA in the seventies, you know. We got nothing else. I know my way round the civil rights movement and that stuff.'

'Okay, keep me in the picture,' the President said, and rang off.

'Watts looks a lot smarter than that prick Svensen,' he said later to a colleague. 'You see – we'll swing this Entakan contract yet.'

'We could use it,' the colleague said. 'The margins are lousy but it should do our cash flow some good.'

The President was pensive. 'On the other hand,' he said, 'I didn't like that stuff about knowing his way around civil rights. We need good company men at Galactic, not goddam pinkos. I must keep an eye on him. And who was the meathead who talked me into granting his stock options?'

Later, while Bill Watts was killing his second evening in the hotel bar, unimagined activity was being generated by his proposal to the Japanese students. For the girl's left faction had decided in a secret caucus meeting of its own that the principle of international solidarity and joint action of all democratic and anti-imperialist forces must prevail. They had therefore instructed the girl to inform the University's Marxist-Leninist cell (Fourth International – Bukharinite faction), of which she was a clandestine member, of the Japanese plans for the

121

Ph.D. ceremony. She was to invite them to organize a mass protest of all other organizations on campus by raising the matter wherever they had infiltrated their members. This was pretty well everywhere short of the Students for a Republican President and the U of SA Bridge Society (here they had no one but they were working on it).

The lobbying, convening of meetings, declaring of quorums and moving of emergency resolutions was now going forward in an atmosphere of mounting moral indignation. The thrill of mass action in an adequately fuzzy and high-sounding cause could be felt rippling and swelling through the campus like a fire spreading through the undergrowth and not yet visible above the trees. The arguments in favour of some kind of action varied sharply with the organization discussing them, and since most of these organizations had no aims in common, this was perhaps not too surprising.

The Save the Earth Society came together in a hastily convened meeting and was addressed by a youth named Zuckmayer. He wore a djellaba and Roman sandals but his heavy horn rims made him look like a dentist from the neck up; the rest being a carpet seller from a Tunisian souk. 'It demands positive action from this organization,' he declared. 'The granting of academic honours to big wheels in the international oil industry legitimizes the rape of our hydro-carbon resources and gives it academic and therefore intellectual and ultimately philosophical respectability.'

'It's bad Karma,' a girl said. She sat cross-legged on the floor, knitting a shapeless item on No. 1 needles which clicked in competition with the speaker.

'The struggle for a sane ecological policy is inseparable from the struggle against big capital.' This from the youth who doubled up membership in the Marxist-Leninists and the Save the Earthers and had introduced the resolution. 'Who's fucking-up the environment if it isn't the forces who control it?'

'Don't they drill for oil in Russia?' someone asked.

'State capitalists,' the youth replied. 'A truly communist society would . . .'

'All right, all right,' the dentist intervened. 'Let's make a little progress here and keep away from politics.'

'You can't keep away from politics,' the youth said. 'It's what Standard Oil wants you to do.'

'Fuck Standard Oil. Let's have a vote here.'

There was unanimity: the Save the Earth Society, U of SA chapter, would protest against the award. They went on to discuss slogans and related matters and elected the girl with the knitting to represent them on a campus-wide Joint Organizing Committee which was to be set up.

The Marxist-Leninists (Fourth International – Bukharinite faction) had altogether more difficulty in working out a correct line. Their chairman was a member of the faculty: a lecturer in Moral Philosophy, under which protective umbrella he gave his students Fanon, Althusser, Lunacharsky and Bukharin as required reading. He had no time for Barthes or Marcuse and had his doubts about the revolutionary thrust of Trotsky, Lenin and Mao Tse-tung. He was still searching for an organization of acceptable revolutionary purity and had become disillusioned with the Marxist-Leninist outfit since they had decided by a narrow majority not to bomb the campus cafeteria as an *acte gratuite* designed to revive the spirit of revolt of the sixties.

'I base my position on Sartre's thesis on necessary violence. What we have here is an opportunity to organize action and therefore to provoke counter-action by the University. They'll call in the National Guard and we'll have Kent State all over, thus exposing the fascist nature of the Board of Regents and the whole academic-industrial complex. It will be highly educative for the masses.'

'Comrade Bukharin taught . . .' an emaciated girl started.

'Bukharin was dealing with the illiterate peasant

123

masses of Tsarist Russia, Marylou,' the chairman said. 'He wasn't dealing with President Harvey Zimmerman or the Arizona State Legislature or *Time* magazine.'

'Yes, comrade, but . . .'

'But the historical context is different. Where's your praxis, Marylou? Watch your predicates. Remember, Marx said history ultimately repeats itself as farce. President Zimmerman is farce. He has nothing in common with the Black Hundreds or the problem of the middle peasants.'

'I guess your attitude is sexist,' Marylou said. 'You think women don't have minds.'

'Some haven't,' the chairman said.

'That's a macho remark, comrade chairperson. It betrays a . . .'

'Why does every discussion have to end up with the women question?' the chairman demanded with a sigh. 'If you were on the barricades for the last assault on the White House, Marylou, I guess you'd ask us to hold it while you analysed the latest communiqué of the Revolutionary Council for male chauvinist deviations. What's more, Bukharin had nothing to say worth listening to on the subject.'

'I read you,' Marylou said, crestfallen.

'Can we return please to important question of General?' asked the Japanese girl. 'We propose mass action to stop award. Does meeting accept?'

They decided on positive action short of serious risk to life, the chairman dissenting. He wanted a small bomb in the amphitheatre, but despite his willingness to bring the calibre down almost to nuisance level only, the meeting limited itself to the offensive use of staves and baseball bats. But they agreed that if the sheriff of Hackberry swore in deputies and armed them, they would arm themselves and exchange fire. They also decided on secret action against the General by the Marxist-Leninists alone on the night before the ceremony, thus breaking the agreement on joint action being reached with all the other organizations. They did this because they had concluded that the Joint Committee's plan was *petit bourgeois* in inspiration and thus, objectively, reactionary. This joint plan was to wait for the ceremony and make it impossible for the award to be made by barracking, unfurling banners, rushing the platform and silencing the mikes. The media would be there to report it all and thus achieve that essential American requirement, maximum communication.

All this, in the view of the chairman of the Marxist-Leninists, was thoroughly reformist and lacking in that uncompromising militancy that would be so educational for the working masses. It wasn't a programme on which the intelligentsia and the oppressed proletariat could unite. They would therefore attack the Guest House at precisely eleven pm, create a maximum disturbance and confront the General in his nightgown with their demands.

These demands were now the subject of bitter ideological debate, from which they emerged sharpened to the point of idiocy and broadened to encompass a fair proportion of the aspirations of every landless peasant in the Third World. The preamble contained a blistering attack on the Soviet Union and some words of guarded approval for Albania. An attempt by Marylou to introduce an analysis of the Nicaraguan situation was defeated on the chairman's ruling that her semantic axis was ill-defined and ultimately bourgeois in content. At this juncture he thought seriously of splitting the organization (itself the result of innumerable factional splits, all related to the need for ideological purity) and forming a Bukharinite-Gaddafi faction. He could see positive aspects in Colonel Gaddafi's anti-imperialist stand in Libya while recognizing the limitations of his class position. But the guy believed in direct action. The chairman had pondered the contradictions inherent in this idea and decided they would form a basis for a useful seminar on the theory of allies in the class struggle. Lenin himself would be a fruitful source. On this question he wasn't such a fool.

The other organizations on campus debated the proposal according to their various lights, nominated their representatives for the Joint Committee and decided on the form their contributions should take.

The Phoenix chapter of the American Nazi Party had infiltrated a member into the Democratic Party at the University. This young man was on the phone to Phoenix that evening, giving the latest information and discussing the kind of counter-demonstration the ANP should mount.

'See the media are told the commies plan to wreck the place,' he said. 'And let the guys in the John Birch Society know too. You need to get plenty of people over here, otherwise the fucking reds will have everything their way.'

A youth belonging to the Save the Earthers, who earned occasional pocket money by phoning the FBI and hoped one day to be a spy, called his Case Officer in Phoenix. 'Thought you'd like to know there's a demonstration planned here against an Indonesian General who's getting a Ph.D. on Monday,' he said.

'Why's that, Jimmy?' asked the Case Officer.

'I'm not too sure but I guess it's because he bosses an oil company which is polluting the sea some place. Maybe the Pacific.'

The Case Officer sighed. 'Thanks, Jimmy. That's great information. Call us if you get the names of the organizers, right?'

'Right, I'll do that.'

'This asshole we have out at Hackberry is useless,' the Case Officer moaned to the man on the next desk. 'I suppose we'd better get a couple of operatives over there to check this thing out. But why can't we find a kid with a few brains? You'd think at a University . . .'

The following day was a Saturday and it was fully taken up with the painting of slogans on boards and banners and the holding of endless meetings of the Joint Committee. Exact details of Monday's ceremony were obtained from Suzie in all innocence. She was delighted and a bit surprised to encounter all this interest on the part of the student body. If only the faculty would do the same . . .

As the news spread through the campus it began to take on a life of its own, growing in scope, acquiring detail and colour, and ultimately undergoing an almost total sea change. By the Sunday, half the students thought General Nasturtion was a wartime collaborator with the Japanese who had supervised the torture of US marines. The other half believed his company was spilling oil into the sea off the Indonesian coast and thereby killing off whole schools of whales. Thus, some saw Monday as a day of protest against man's inhumanity to man, allied to the struggle against fascism and imperialism. Whereas the other half saw it as a protest against man's inhumanity to whales and other similarly fashionable creatures, allied to a perfectly reasonable and strikingly apposite demand that the earth's limited resources be recaptured from the money-crazed oil companies and – by a logical extension – the multinationals in general. This confusion of data and thus of aims found its reflection in the bewildering range of slogans being devised for the morrow.

The Japanese, of course, saw the General as an anti-Japanese fascist, and the handful of Africans from Zanzibar, labouring under an inadequate command of English and confusing Indonesia with India, thought the campus was about to receive the visit of an Indian business millionaire of some kind, thus affording them an opportunity to demonstrate their deep bias against Indians and particularly meal merchants and traders in such necessities as cloth, household supplies and groceries.

But there was unity in one respect: the General was not to receive his Doctorate at Hackberry.

A quiet girl who had been nominated to the Joint Committee from a body dedicated to the legalization of hallucinogens asked whether it wouldn't be best to send a deputation to President Zimmerman demanding cancellation of the programme. The idea was received in stunned silence, since what the militants wanted was confrontation and not negotiation. There hadn't been an issue as pregnant with possibilities as the General for a long time, since he could be adjusted to mean all things to almost anyone on campus. They were not going to let him be filched from them at this late stage.

'You're stoned, Joanne,' someone said. 'You're talking balls.'

Joanne giggled. 'I may be stoned a little bit,' she said, 'but I guess the President would listen to reason. After all, he doesn't want the place all smashed up.'

'I get good vibes from what Joanne's saying,' the girl with the knitting said. 'I dig meeting the President.'

'I can get behind it,' a young man from the Drama Group chipped in. 'Why not give the guy a chance to be a human being?'

'That's what they'd like you to do,' someone else said. 'If we let them meet our demands we'll end with some lousy compromise and the people get screwed again. We're always giving these bastards chances. Who the hell wants to negotiate with that asshole Zimmerman?'

No one cared to admit wanting anything of the kind and Joanne's proposal died of neglect.

The Borkh twins had been given detailed instructions by Nicos Papadopoulos: they were to catch an early afternoon flight out of LA to Phoenix and make their connection to Flagstaff, where a limo would be waiting to take them to the Holiday Inn at Hackberry. There they were to await the arrival of the others an hour or two later. Papadopoulos had explained it all in German and with some misgivings: the girls were not very bright, had no English at all, and seemed to him perfectly capable of flying off somewhere else if the offer were good enough. But they nodded vigorously at all he said and he left them clutching their airline tickets and a piece of paper on which he had written in English some of the essential data of their journey. 'It may lead them to the University,' he said afterwards to George Pidduck, 'and then again it may not. My judgment is that if they meet a couple of college quarter-backs or even a pair of Chinese waiters of the right size, they'll be lost to us.'

But Waldtraute and Sieglinde had duly arrived at LA airport and found their way to the correct gate. They were sitting in the lounge waiting for their flight to be called when a guttural cry rang out from the check-in counter.

It was Hildegarde, dishevelled and bewildered by endless hours of flying from Jakarta and fresh from a baffling but finally successful encounter with the US Immigration Service. They fell on each other in a flurry of exclamations and cries of affection.

'Why are you here?'

'I can't tell you. Not now. Maybe later.'

'We're so happy to see you.'

'Me too. How has it been?'

'All right. Disgusting but all right.' They all laughed. 'We like Beverly Hills.'

'It's very high class,' Sieglinde said.

'She likes the shops,' Waldtraute explained, 'and the food. She loves the food.'

'Wonderful! They have pie shops with forty different kinds of pie,' Sieglinde said. 'I had chocolate pecan. Also blueberry. And the ice-cream! My God, I had chocolate mint chip with banana and whipped cream on top. Fantastic!'

'Where is the General?'

'He follows on a later flight.'

'And the Englishman?'

'Ah, ha,' Sieglinde cried, 'so that's why you're here!' She was not at all dull when it came to sex.

Hildegarde grinned. 'He's wonderful,' she said simply.

They travelled happily on to Phoenix and Flagstaff, chattering noisily all the way. 'You mustn't tell anyone I'm here,' Hildegarde warned. 'Especially not the General. He'd be very angry and would send me away from Jakarta.'

'Don't worry,' Sieglinde said, 'we shan't say a word, will we?'

'Not a word. But you'd better be careful. The fat Greek told us the Holiday Inn is the only hotel in Hackberry, so you'll have to stay there too, and that means you must keep out of sight when the beastly little man visits us to be pumped full of water.'

'Like filling a hot water bottle,' Sieglinde said.

'Or pumping up a beach ball.'

'Give me a bondage freak any day.'

'Ugh! I hate all that rubber. It makes me sweat.'

'Yes, but it's somehow more decent.'

'I think I prefer chocolate pecan.'

The gusts of peasant laughter could be heard in First Class and someone called for a little silence. They chortled and dug at each other with their big fists and Sieglinde streaked her eye make-up and had to remake her face. Time passed pleasantly through the flight and the hot drive to Hackberry.

At the hotel Hildegarde undertook the checking in and found herself pitting her German syntax against the heavy drawl of the country girl at the desk. While the unravelling took place, the twins wandered over to inspect the bar. Seated none too securely on a tall stool, Bill Watts was looking moodily into his fifth double bourbon of the afternoon and dreaming, if not of home, then of some other place than Hackberry. He looked up to see, through an alcoholic haze, two dramatically outsized blondes of absolutely identical aspect, down to their handbags and hairbands.

'I don't believe it,' he muttered. 'I simply don't believe it. I can't be drunk enough to mistake one regular-size chick for this. Wow!' And he climbed off his stool and advanced unsteadily towards them. As he did so, a third blonde of similar dimensions and general appearance made her way from the lobby and joined the pair who had briefly frightened him into thinking that the booze had got to him at last and left him with double vision.

'Christ!' he said. 'Place is alive with them. Boy, is this

130

going to be a great evening.'

The girls looked at him approaching and, unaccustomed to evading the attentions of any man until they could assess his merits, gave him three encouraging smiles.

'Hi, girls,' he said. The liquor had not sharpened his vocabulary.

'Hallo,' the third girl said.

'You arrived – just arrived?' He waved in the direction of the lobby.

'Yes, from LA we come out.'

'LA – better than this dump. Terrible dump, this dump.' He steadied himself against a pillar. 'I'm very glad to see you. Name's Bill – Bill Watts, from Fort Worth, Texas. Better place than this dump. You from LA?'

'No, we are German girls.'

'Why you in this dump – all way from Germany for Chrissakes?'

'For ceremony tomorrow we come.'

He tried to focus on each of them in turn, fearful that he would be confronted with six images. Then he let out a mirthless laugh. 'Cerem – ceremony t'morrow, eh? Some party that'll be!' He gave a very slow and knowing wink. 'My advice,' he said, leaning dangerously towards Hildegarde, 'my advice – don't go. Not safe for a gorgeous chick like you – and you – and you.' He pointed vaguely to each of them in turn.

'Why not?' Hildegarde asked. But Bill Watts's mind was dimly perceiving other possibilities. 'You have dinner with me t'night?' he asked, directing his question collectively towards the three of them.

They conferred in German. 'Maybe,' Hildegarde said. 'But maybe our friends arrive.'

'Have a drink now,' Bill Watts said. 'C'mon, have a drink.'

'First I go to my room,' Hildegarde said.

'You two, you have a drink,' he demanded.

The twins giggled and nodded. 'Vodka-coke,' they said in unison. '*Mitt Eis*.'

CHAPTER
12

It might be supposed, with the concentration in Hackberry, Arizona, of virtually all the *dramatis personae* in the drama of the Entakan contract, that it would be in Hackberry that the question would finally be resolved one way or the other. The supposition would be a natural one: for was not General Nasturtion present – the man who alone made all the big decisions at Entakan? Were not the British there, in the shape of one extremely supple and devious Indonesian, an even more astute Greek, and an Englishman who was not, when it came to it, a complete bloody fool? And the Americans, if not there in force, had a competent man on the spot – intoxicated but active – while away in Fort Worth the President of Galactic pursued his game plan like any commander back at base. It would seem, too, that all the bit players were waiting in the wings, ready to come in on cue in the unfolding drama: the three German tarts, one of them bursting with her dramatic news for her Englishman; the students in their multifarious organizations; the Nazis and their allies preparing to set out from Phoenix and other towns which had been alerted; the forces of law and order (yet to become aware of the riot being organized under their noses); and of course the media. Strutting in his elevator cowboy boots in the still centre of this explosive mixture which was due to go critical at any moment was President Harvey Zimmerman, Head of the University, a businessman chasing $250,000 less twenty per cent like a stoat after a rabbit and unaware that the warren was about to collapse and bury him at any moment.

It is a fair supposition, then, that out of such a situation a resolution would be found. But life is rarely that simple. Not that there was anything strikingly simple about the situation on that Sunday afternoon as the Nasturtion party drove in four hired limousines across the scrub and desert between Flagstaff and Hackberry.

No, it is necessary for a proper understanding of what happened later to leave the actors in Hackberry rehearsing their lines and adjusting their costumes, as it were, before curtain-up, and consider what had been happening in the past week in, of all places, Tokyo. Here, a week before the fateful weekend of preparations for the Ph.D. ceremony, a meeting had taken place in the office of the Deputy Minister for International Trade in charge of Asian and Australasian Affairs. Present at the meeting were Mr Sanjiro Konoda of Kawama Industries, the chairman of the Imperial Bank of Tokyo, the Deputy Minister himself and two silent and bespectacled young men who took notes of everything that was said. All those in the Deputy Minister's office, without exception, were related to each other. The Deputy Minister was the cousin of Mr Konoda's wife and the chairman of the bank was his uncle. The young men were nephews of the Deputy Minister. These family ties, while not decisive in decision-taking, nevertheless helped to engender mutual confidence and a willingness to perform favours, one for the other. A feudal pattern of relationships and obligations had been spatchcocked into the fabric of a modern industrial state, and who was to say it didn't have tangible advantages?

Pale, unsweetened tea was served in shallow bowls and steaming face towels were distributed and collected. When they were settled, the Deputy Minister opened the proceedings with some complimentary remarks about his guests, coupled with humble thanks for coming to see him. He invited the chairman of the bank to speak.

'In the case of the Entakan default we are confronted with a difficult situation, as you know,' the chairman said. 'But as often happens, difficult situations can provide excellent opportunities if one acts resolutely and with correct timing. I humbly suggest we have such an opportunity here.'

The others nodded. The young men bent over their notebooks, their tea untasted. 'My bank, together with three associated Japanese banks, are creditors of Entakan to the extent of something over $940 millions. As you know, Entakan have defaulted on interest and capital repayment in the current month. We believe they will default again next month.'

'Will they collapse?' the Deputy Minister asked.

'No, the Indonesian Government will not let them and in any case the Western banks will not push matters that far. Nor will we, of course, but I see no reason why we should not be very firm with these people.'

'You mean . . .?'

'I mean that we should make it clear that we would have no hesitation in forcing a receivership if there is not a complete refinancing of the loans, tied to an Indonesian Government guarantee, plus certain other conditions.'

'Will the Western banks follow such a line?'

The chairman shook his head. 'They have already decided, as you know, not to press hard. That is because they have no muscle. But we here in Japan have all the muscle we need, since we are the main customers for a wide range of Indonesian exports, including oil. My proposal is that we should now use this muscle and that the thing is best done at Government level.'

'An interesting idea,' the Deputy Minister said. 'I imagine that is why we are honoured with Mr Konoda's presence.'

'Precisely,' the chairman said. 'I took the liberty of asking you to receive Mr Konoda with me because his company has been tendering for a $16 million contract with Entakan, so far without success. He believes that an immediate intervention at Government level could change that situation. For my part, I would regard it as a test of our ability to use Entakan's default to strengthen our trading position in a number of ways.'

The Deputy Minister nodded. 'But would the Indonesian Government be able to control this General who is said to run Entakan as if it belonged to him?'

'A very pertinent point,' the chairman replied, 'to which the answer is almost certainly negative. My proposal is therefore that our Government's demand to the Indonesians should be that General Nasturtion has to go: otherwise we will take all legal steps to enforce the terms of our loans to the letter. I would humbly suggest that such a demand be linked to the granting of the oil servicing contract to Mr Konoda's company, who are honoured clients of my bank and eminently capable of performing satisfactorily for Entakan. Other concessions by Entakan to our trading companies can of course be negotiated later.'

'May I respectfully add,' Mr Konoda broke in, 'that we need to move with all possible speed. Within a week the contract will be awarded to the British.'

'You have tendered in due form?'

'Certainly. Our bid can be defended despite the deliberately confusing terms of Entakan's original specifications.'

The Deputy Minister nodded. 'The idea is interesting. I will discuss it with my colleagues and I will let you know what is decided. I can do that by tomorrow. Then, if we accept this course of action, we shall have to see what can be done in the next few days. It will be difficult but perhaps not impossible.'

They bowed and smiled their way out and the Deputy Minister went along the corridor to report to his chief, the Minister for International Trade & Industry.

Three days later a meeting took place in the office of the Indonesian Prime Minister in Jakarta. Face required that no one make demands, that no one resist those unspoken demands, and that no one show any emotion stronger than surprise or the mildest of pained feelings, provoked no doubt by a misunderstanding of a regrett-able kind. The conversation therefore proceeded like a trussed chicken trying to cross a farmyard, and what could and should have been a flaming twenty-minute row extended under the weight of circumlocution to a tedious two hours. Any fly on the wall would have concluded that nothing had been truly asked and nothing granted – certainly that nothing whatever had been settled between the parties.

The fly would have been wrong. For the Japanese delegation had, for Japanese, been unusually frank and forthright and the Indonesians, for Indonesians, had been exceptionally angry and stubborn. No one made anything remotely resembling an overt threat, yet threats of an indirect kind were understood. No one said General Nasturtion must go, but why say as much if the demand can be conveyed in a lifted eyebrow and a polite enquiry about the General's health and the competence of his deputy? The Japanese Minister of Finance, no less, headed the Japanese delegation and his presence was meant (and was understood) to underline the seriousness with which the Japanese Government viewed Entakan's financial improvidence. But throughout the meeting he uttered not a word other than 'Good morning' and 'Goodbye', since his presence was deemed to say in itself all the Japanese wished to convey. Any attempt to spell the thing out could be construed as ill-mannered and grasping.

What talking there was on the Japanese side was done by the Ambassador and the chairman of the Imperial Bank of Tokyo. The Indonesians favoured long silences, broken by expressions of undying respect and willingness to do all to make their guests contented. As a contribution to the drama of the Entakan contract it could all be said to be highly allusive and indirect. But if one considers vectors of forces bearing on a problem, this was a vector all right. In due time it would make itself felt, though perhaps not in quite the way that the chairman of the Japanese bank had had in mind.

When the Japanese were driving away from the meeting, after taking tea and working their way through a series of ceremonious farewells, the Minister of Finance grunted. 'Useful,' he said. 'Make these wretches pay up. We can squeeze a lot out of them on the trading side, starting with the contract for the oil rigs. And see that poisonous snake Nasturtion is kicked out. I want a reliable man at Entakan who understands Japanese rights and aspirations.' He hawked noisily and spat into his handkerchief.

Meanwhile, the Indonesian Prime Minister was in conference with his Minister of Mines, who was laughingly held to be in political charge of Entakan and thus of General Nasturtion. The Minister was a former General of Artillery and this helped him to understand Nasturtion, whom he'd known since their days together in the campaign of the Fifties. 'We can't touch him,' he said now to the Prime Minister. 'He keeps files on everyone.'

'On you?'

The Minister shrugged expressively and allowed himself a weak smile.

'On me?'

He shrugged again but didn't risk the smile. 'Do you think it matters?'

'I think so. With a man like that.'

'On the other hand, the Japanese can make things very difficult for us.'

'I appreciate that.'

They sat in silence, wrestling with the dilemma.

'I think,' said the Minister of Mines, 'that the Japanese might settle for a compromise. If we persuaded Entakan to grant this contract to Kawama Industries and maybe conceded some points in next year's trade agreement, then they may drop the question of Nasturtion and take a more patient line on Entakan's default.'

'I will talk to Nasturtion,' the Prime Minister said. 'Where is he?'

'In Arizona.'

'Where did you say?'

'Arizona, USA. He is receiving an honorary Doctorate at a university there.'

'My God, the man's crazy. His company is in financial crisis, with the banks out for the kill, and he goes off to collect some idiotic honour.'

'It was arranged by the British to reward his services in granting them this contract.'

The Prime Minister buried his head in his hands and sighed deeply. 'I don't suppose,' he said, 'that with Nasturtion over there in the USA, you could . . . perhaps . . . that is, if you know the location of these files . . .'

The Minister shook his head. 'I am afraid not. You can be sure they are in a safe place. Perhaps with his lawyer in Geneva.'

'He has a personal lawyer there?'

'He has lawyers in many places. Also bank accounts.'

They relapsed into silence. 'When does he get back?' the Prime Minister asked.

'He gets his Ph.D. at a ceremony on Monday and plans to return the following Monday via New York and Paris.'

'Call him and tell him to come straight back after this ceremony. Say we have a crisis on our hands and tell him not to sign with the British until he has seen me.'

'Respectfully, I beg you to be careful how you handle him. He is a dangerous man.'

'I know that,' the Prime Minister said ruefully. 'I will do what I can, which may not be much. But perhaps the danger of Entakan's financial situation will persuade him. His lawyer in Geneva won't have any files to deal with *that*.'

CHAPTER
13

'I was not satisfied, Sombolon, with the press at Phoenix airport.' General Nasturtion had Mr Sombolon next to him in the back of the big Cadillac as they drove through the blistering afternoon heat of the Arizona desert towards Hackberry.

'That was not intended to be major coverage,' Mr Sombolon said nimbly. 'All the important newspapers and TV networks will cover the ceremony itself.'

'There were no television cameras.'

'They will be at the ceremony.'

'Even so, a youth in jeans and a half-naked girl – I do not call that a press conference, even in America.'

'That young man represented the *New York Times*,' Mr Sombolon lied.

'I doubt it,' the General said. 'When he asked me a question he said, "Our readers in Phoenix would like to know . . ." That does not sound like the *New York Times*. And the girl said she represented something called *Lick*. What the hell is that?'

'It is a leading US magazine, General.' Mr Sombolon was lying again. *Lick* was an underground bi-weekly which combined radical politics biased towards the Third World with a sexual emancipation platform which would make a New Orleans madam blench. Mr Sombolon had bought a copy at the airport and after glancing through it had hastily disposed of it in the men's toilet.

'Get me a copy,' the General said.

'Certainly, General.' Mr Sombolon would die before handing such a publication to the General, whose vastly inflated sense of personal dignity would certainly not permit him to appear alongside articles on the joys of animalism without creating an almighty fuss about it.

The General turned to other matters. 'What are the sleeping arrangements, Sombolon?'

'The University has a most excellent Guest House for distinguished visitors. There they are the personal guests of the University President,' Mr Sombolon replied. 'You and your party will stay there. I and my associates and the Indonesian journalists will be at the Holiday Inn hotel which I understand is a mile from the campus.'

'And what about the German twins?'

'They are also at the hotel. It was the only place to put them. But it is most discreet. Being in fact an American-style motel, you can reach their room direct without going through the hotel lobby. You will have a local taxi available to take you there and return you to the Guest House at any hour. I believe the arrangements will be very satisfactory for you.'

'I hope so, Sombolon. I intend to visit them this evening. Please let them know.'

'Of course. I will see that everything is in order and I will let you have their room number.'

'And tomorrow?'

'In the morning President Zimmerman will take you on a tour of inspection of the University. He will then entertain you and your party to lunch, and at 2 pm the award will be made. I understand they have a large open amphitheatre and there will be at least a thousand people present.' Mr Sombolon had invented this figure. It was a good example of his carefree way with untruths, since he had no idea what he would say if the audience turned out to be fifty reluctant undergraduates.

The General's motorcade was now approaching the campus. Soon it reached the gates and passed under a streamer proclaiming WELCOME GENERAL NASTUR-TIUM TO U OF SA! The signwriter's error had been inadvertent and its rather charming meaning was fortunately lost on the General himself. Mr Sombolon had had a nasty moment: the General's name had been a rather dim house joke at All World Oil Services for years.

The four limousines drove on through the strangely quiet and deserted campus, with scarcely a student to be seen, until they reached the Guest House. At the entrance stood President Harvey Zimmerman with Suzie at his side. He had dressed for the occasion in a suit of heavily slubbed raw silk in blinding white with the trousers cut snug to the hips and slightly flared at the bottoms and the jacket with narrow lapels, cut long, one button and with patch pocket picked out in black saddle stitching. He wore black-and-white patent elevators, a silk button-down shirt in a startling shade of purple, and a white tie with the University's crest emblazoned upon it. There was a good deal of gold glistening at his wrists and fingers. His deeply tanned con man's face and *faux-naif* mop of white hair, emerging from all this finery, completed the thoroughly spurious impression – from which the General was fortunately shielded by the cultural chasm separating Indonesia from Southern Arizona.

Suzie was in a flowing shift of pinkish voile through which her magnificent body could be apprehended when she moved. She had woven her mane of blonde hair into a magnificent cottage loaf atop her head. As the General alighted first from the car, she flashed him her healthiest and most beguiling smile. 'Why, honey,' she said to the President, 'isn't he just the cutest thing? I know I'm simply going to adore him.'

The General, catching sight of Suzie, immediately concluded that she had been courteously supplied by the University's Board of Regents for his private use during his stay. This would have been the case in the East, but he reflected that they would have had more tact than to parade the girl publicly like this, with his wife and children about to follow him out of the car. It confirmed yet again his low opinion of Western manners. Furthermore, he would have to find some way of getting rid of her, since his sexual interests lay entirely with the German twins. He would leave it to Sombolon to tell the President without offence that he did not after all need the services of a woman, though he would readily admit that the one provided was a magnificent specimen. All this he settled in his mind as he walked up the steps and bowed courteously towards the gaily clad figure of Harvey Zimmerman and tried to crease his face into a smile.

Introductions made, Mr Sombolon joined George Pidduck and the others in the fourth car, which drove on to the Holiday Inn. There the party were checked in and awarded their room keys. Mr Sombolon enquired after the Borkh twins. 'I guess they're in the bar,' the reception girl said. He went across and found them there, each with the latest of a string of vodka-and-cokes in her hand, one on either side of an almost insensible Bill Watts, wedged upright between them. Each of his hands was attempting to grasp a huge thigh, and bereft of a third hand with which to raise his latest bourbon to his lips, and unwilling to abandon his hold on either twin, he was puzzling happily over his dilemma. The twins, less drunk but scarcely sober, were chattering and laughing across to each other in their native tongue. They recognized Mr Sombolon and waved at him happily. Then they got up. Deprived of their support on either side, Bill Watts keeled over to his left and promptly fell asleep along the bench they had all been sitting at.

Using a mixture of simplified English, a word or two of German and many gestures, Mr Sombolon conveyed the news that the General would visit them in their room that evening. He was not happy about their state of intoxication: on both moral and practical grounds it seemed to him deplorable. He hoped they would sober up in time for the General's arrival.

George Pidduck and Nicos Papadopoulos had made their way to their rooms, and as Pidduck was inserting his key in the lock, Hildegarde came out of the next room, intending to join the twins in the bar. Catching sight of her beloved Englishman, she let out a shriek which echoed alarmingly along the corridor, and taking the few steps that separated them at a lumbering trot, flung her arms around him and clasped him to her bosom, collapsing his lungs and causing him to gasp for air.

'*Ach, mein Putzi!*' she cried.

'What on earth are you doing in Arizona?' Pidduck exclaimed.

'I come to you,' Hildegarde said. 'I come to *mein* Englishman, *ja*, because I have the important news.'

'You mean to say you've followed me all the way out here to *tell* me something?'

'*Ja, ja*, very important. Also, of *mein Putzi* I have been dreaming, no? And so, to myself I say, "This big news you have. Also you like to make love again." So I come.'

'All right,' Pidduck said, 'you'd better come in and tell me what it's all about.' He didn't know whether he was pleased or horrified to see her.

She followed him into his room, and looking at his big frame and the rugged, bronzed face with the interesting eyes and sensuous mouth, she told herself yet again that this time she was in love.

'So,' George Pidduck said, 'what's this news of yours that you had to bring half way round the world?'

'It is of the Americans who also the Entakan contract are wanting.'

'You mean Galactic?'

'*Ja, ja*, that is the name. In Jakarta I was meeting a black American who tells me they have plans for the contract winning.'

'What plans?'

'He tells me they play few tricks in Arizona and spoil the party.'

'Is that what he said?'

'*Ja*, he said.'

'Did he now! And how exactly are they going to spoil the party?'

'That I do not know. But the black American, he was

very sure. He was saying contract will not go to Britishers.'

'Is that all you know?'

'That is all. Is that useful?'

'Yes, I think so. It was a nice thing to do – coming all this way to tell me.'

'You make your Hildegarde a present for information?' She might love this man, but a deal was a deal.

'Of course. Leave that to me.'

She smiled at him. 'What a wonderful man,' she thought, as Pidduck called Mr Sombolon on the house phone and told him to come over right away.

Mr Sombolon's surprise at seeing Hildegarde was mingled with alarm. The situation, he felt, was complicated and dangerous enough already, what with the drunken twins reeling around the bar. Anything calculated to make it more so must be bad, and there was no doubt at all that Hildegarde with her present tenacity and powerful erotic fixation on George Pidduck was a complicating factor of some moment. What if the General caught sight of her? What if, in her impassioned frame of mind, she was thwarted, turned nasty and decided to tell the General all? Mr Sombolon could immediately see a dozen appalling scenarios waiting to be written. And in none of them could he see any material advantage to himself.

George Pidduck gave him Hildegarde's news. He pondered it for a long while, holding the tips of his slender fingers together, his shrewd and mistrustful eyes half closed. 'We are facing greatest dangers,' he said at last. 'I have much unhappiness over situation.'

'Perhaps we should warn the General that the Yanks are up to no good. At least, if something goes wrong, he won't switch the contract to them.'

'But my humble suggestion, please, is in that case he may go to damn French again or to damn bloody Japanese.'

'I can't see him going back to the French after the way you genned him up on the Legion of Honour.'

'With the General, excuse me please, it is rarely possible to make best predictions,' Mr Sombolon said. 'Also, he hates Japanese, but for suitable gift he certainly gives them contract. His principle is always business first. We are in very damn dangerous situation, I think.'

'But at least,' Pidduck said, 'we know, thanks to Hildegarde here, that something's brewing. What we have to do before tomorrow is find out what it is.'

Mr Sombolon bowed his head in a gesture of deep respect designed to mask his contempt for the Englishman's analysis of the problem. 'All your sayings on this matter are very wise and most wonderfully valuable,' he said. Foolishness, he believed, must be flattered lest one's impatience with it be noticed and resented. 'But I beg to confess,' he continued, 'that in my humble lack of wisdom I do not know in what way to discover these American plans.'

'Nor do I yet,' Pidduck said, 'but we have a few hours to work on it.'

Hildegarde was listening to the exchange and trying to follow it. She was dimly aware that her news had produced something like consternation. Therefore, it was solid news, worthy of a fair reward and surely sufficient to arouse in her Englishman's breast those feelings of gratitude and approval which could find their expression, later, in bed. All this was good. What was not so good was that her Englishman appeared puzzled and distressed. And so she badly wanted to help. But how? Who in this place might know what these tricks of the black man's might be? Whom did she know here? No one, except the drunk from Texas. And because she wanted so badly to help and had nothing but this drunk to contribute, she contributed him.

'Down in bar,' she said, 'I am meeting drunk man from Texas coming. I am telling him I go tomorrow to ceremony and he is winking so and telling not to go.' She imitated Bill Watts' wink.

'Where in Texas?'

145

'I remember not,' Hildegarde said, crestfallen. 'A name with two words. You tell me names, I tell you yes, no.'

Pidduck hit it at once. 'Fort Worth?'

'That is it!'

'It must be one of the Galactic mob,' Pidduck said to Mr Sombolon.

'Maybe we can get him to talk.'

'He is drunk,' Hildegarde said. 'Perhaps now very drunk.'

'So what can we do?'

Mr Sombolon looked pensively at Hildegarde. 'With humble excusings I have plan.'

'What is it, Mr Sombolon?'

'In my plan, Miss Glauber here will offer this man good services – you understand, of private nature – and in his room if he is truly drunk then he will sleep and she will bring his papers to us. That is my humble plan.'

'Do you understand?' Pidduck asked Hildegarde.

'*Ja*, I understand. Is good. For you, I do this.' And she gave him a look of unbridled adoration.

'Okay,' Pidduck said, 'you go ahead now and I'll be in my room whenever you've got anything to show me.'

It was less than an hour later, a little after 7 pm, that Hildegarde knocked on Pidduck's door. He let her in. She was carrying a thick folder which she put on the table. 'I do not understand these writings so I bring all papers from his briefcase,' she said.

'Is he asleep?'

'Like the baby.'

'Did you have to . . .?'

'*Nein*. Too drunk.'

Pidduck opened the folder and started reading. Most of it consisted of the sheets of paper on which the quotations from General Nasturtion's speeches had been written. Many were identified by time and place. It didn't take long for him to divine what they were. On one sheet were three Japanese names – the names of the three students – and a campus address. Putting two

146

and two together, Pidduck rapidly made four. 'Okay,' he said, 'I'm going to photocopy all this downstairs, then I'll want you to put it back where you found it. Do you have his key?'

Hildegarde nodded. She was enjoying the excitement but wished things wouldn't move so fast.

Later, the papers copied and restored to the sleeping man's briefcase, Pidduck sat with Nicos Papadopoulos and Mr Sombolon debating the next move. 'It looks as if Galactic have persuaded the Jap students to wreck the ceremony tomorrow,' he said. 'That would screw both us and the Japs and leave Galactic in command of the field, the only ones with clean hands. What happens if we take the evidence to the General?'

'Excuse me, please,' Mr Sombolon said. 'Permit me to explain Indonesian viewing of life. For General Nasturtion, most important matter is money. Also most important matter is face. So my understandings are these: if our excellent company organized ceremony and ceremony is big bloody messing up, then General loses much face and responsibility is our company who organized these things. General not interested in whose fault. Interest only in what happens. And what happens is General showing much foolishness in *New York Times*.'

'So what would he do next?'

'If he believes story, he will grant contract to Japanese. If he does not believe, he will grant to Americans. Unfortunately, not possible to foresee which way General may decide. That is always difficult matter. General is impatient man. Often is not listening.'

'Can we stop these crazy Japs?' Papadopoulos asked. 'Talk to them or something?'

Mr Sombolon shook his head sadly. 'Japanese students not interested in reasoning. If they organize demonstration they are only interested in demonstration, not in reason for it. Excuse me, I do not think it possible to show these students that General Nasturtion is not anti-Japanese. The reason is simple, he *is* anti-Japanese. Oh, most highly.'

147

'Can we get Zimmerman to call in the cops and get the ceremony protected? suggested Papadopoulos.

'We could,' Pidduck said, 'but that would guarantee a riot and even worse publicity. I should think it's just what these people want.' They argued on through dinner and neither Pidduck nor Papadopoulos noticed an unusually absent and thoughtful look in Mr Sombolon's eyes.

At ten o'clock that evening the General summoned the taxi which had been reserved for him and directed the driver to take him to the Holiday Inn. The driver, a moonlighting student of Comparative Religion and dedicated member of the Marxist-Leninists, was deeply disturbed by this development, bearing in mind the plans he and his colleagues had made for the General later that evening. But he drove his cab over to the Holiday Inn, and when he reached it the General made his understandable but fatal mistake. 'Return for me at midnight,' he said. 'Please knock on the door of Room 72 and I will come out.'

'Okay,' the student of Comparative Religion said, and as the General moved round to the side of the building in search of Room 72, he got out of his cab and went to the phone in the hotel lobby. He got through to a fellow militant and explained what had happened.

'No sweat,' the fellow militant said, 'we switch the operation to the hotel. On the stroke of eleven, right?'

'Right.'

'Room 72?'

'Room 72.' The student of Comparative Religion went back to his cab. Was this how it had been as they synchronized their watches for the storming of the Winter Palace?

Meanwhile, in Room 72 the Borkh twins had made themselves ready for the General save in one respect. The administering of a high colonic irrigation – to dwell for a moment on a necessary if distasteful technicality – requires much the same measure of dexterity and

148

control as, say, the inserting of a key in a lock and the regulating of any flow of liquid. If one is untrained in the procedures and has only limited practice to draw upon, that is obstacle enough. But if one has been drinking vodka-and-cokes for several hours past and is, if not completely smashed, at any rate stupidly drunk, then the task of administering a successful high colonic to an impatient, irritable and grossly over-excited Asian tycoon becomes a daunting one indeed and fraught with risk of error. This was the situation of the twins as the General removed his clothes and, in a poverty-stricken kind of foreplay, started grabbing at any parts of the twins' anatomy which protruded and upon which he could obtain a purchase. The fact of their drunkenness escaped him for some time since they had no language in common with him and he was in any case familiar with the mindless giggling and bursts of unmotivated laughter of the German girls. Then, towards eleven o'clock, unaware of the significance of the hour, he turned on his side and signalled Waldtraute to proceed with the real business of the evening.

Sieglinde in the bathroom had filled the container with water which was scaldingly hot, and in a fit of drunken abandon she had emptied into it half a bottle of suntan lotion. 'Like that, he won't get sunburned up there,' she cried. 'Shall we put in some eau de cologne to make him smell sweet?'

'Good idea,' Waldtraute said. They added it in.

'And some coke in case he's thirsty?'

'Aren't you clever!' Waldtraute said. They added Coca-Cola. There was vodka in it. Then, laughing uproariously, they brought the strange brew out of the bathroom and prepared to administer it to the impatient General.

'What's this ridiculous joke?' he asked, irritated by the delay and the suspicion that the twins were laughing at him. But they didn't understand his question. Waldtraute couldn't keep her hand steady or her eyes properly focused and so had some difficulty with the nozzle, but it finally found its target and the valve having been opened, the noxious mixture was fed into the General. It was a few moments before the excessive heat of the water communicated itself to him. Then he let out a howl in which Professor Sigmund Freud's pain and pleasure principle became operative. The General found himself in the classic bind of the sadomasochist: he was loving what he hated. The ultimate effects, such as they might be, of the suntan lotion, eau de cologne, Coca-Cola and vodka were not yet making themselves felt.

The strange ritual was taking its course, the General meanwhile becoming aware of an unwonted internal discomfort and putting this down to the fact that the water was clearly hotter than usual. But, perversely, this added discomfort seemed to add to his excitement. He was certainly not complaining. Meanwhile, the twins tried to contain their mirth and speculated drunkenly in German on the effects their new enema mixture would produce.

'It will make him ill,' Waldtraute said. 'It will poison his gut.'

'I hope so.'

'That isn't kind.'

'Then we'll have some peace and can have some fun together. I feel like it.'

'So do I.'

When the liquid had all been transferred from the container to the General, Waldtraute said briskly, like some District Nurse, 'Okay – finish. *Ist gutt?*'

'Yes, yes,' the General said. 'You can remove the nozzle now.' He was feeling extraordinarily uncomfortable. Cramps of an unusual kind were beginning to trouble him. He feared he would have to cut short his pleasure. And it was just as Waldtraute had withdrawn the nozzle that a sound as of a modest riot was heard outside the window and an insistent and clearly ill-intentioned banging began on the door. The Marxist-Leninists (Fourth International – Buhkarinite faction) had arrived, fifteen strong and five minutes late but imbued with insurrectionary fervour and brandishing placards proclaiming: *LAND TO THE PEASANTS * DEATH TO THE OLIGARCHIES * NASTURTION MUST GO!*

This last among a set of difficult demands was perhaps the most intractable. For as the hubbub outside increased in intensity and the banging on the door resounded through the room, the General had sprung naked and grossly distended from the bed and made for the bathroom. It was not that he was afraid: he was, if anything, a courageous man. It was simply that someone in his condition faced an urgent and overwhelming requirement before he could tackle ill-wishers or whoever it might prove to be. And as he set about this perfectly natural function, he was at first puzzled and then horrified to discover that natural as it might be, it was a function he was presently unable to perform.

Whether it was the effect of the concoction within or the riot without, some muscular spasm appeared to have occurred: slogan or no slogan, the General could *not* go! Furthermore, the lotion or maybe the eau de cologne or possibly the Coca-Cola and vodka was now having its full effect. The General's fundament was in spasm and he was in agony. And it was in this situation that the drunken twins, mystified but not alarmed by the racket outside, opened the door, crying '*Kommen-sie herein!*'

The fifteen people who now burst into the room, chanting slogans and waving ill-spelt banners, were not deterred by the sight of two large blondes, naked and foolishly drunk. 'Christ,' someone said, 'there's nothing but hookers in these hotels nowadays.'

With no Indonesian army general in sight, they proceeded to the bathroom. The door was locked. They battered upon it and the taxi driver, who was among them, shouted 'No academic honours for the oppressors!' through the keyhole. By now the General was writhing miserably on the floor, his sexual appetite utterly quenched. The advance of the enemy to the bathroom itself seemed to prolong his muscular spasm and the twins' appalling hot toddy was firmly bottled up inside him.

The noise in Room 72 could be clearly heard in 71 across the corridor.

'What on earth is that racket?' George Pidduck asked.

Hildegarde, whose mouth once again was full, mumbled incoherently and went on with what she was doing. She had little ability to encompass two thoughts at once, nor did she find it easy to switch her attention quickly from one activity to another. In any case, she was perfectly happy with her present task and prided herself on doing it with exceptional skill. She could hear the racket outside but it did not interest her.

'Hey, stop that a minute, will you, there's a riot out there,' George Pidduck said. But Hildegarde only grunted and shook her head vigorously. 'Ow, careful!' Pidduck cried. 'For God's sake stop a minute. I think the Indians are back in Arizona.'

Reluctantly, Hildegarde looked up. 'What is this with Indians?' she asked.

'Never mind,' Pidduck said, getting off the bed and pulling on a dressing gown. 'I'd better see what the hell's going on. You stay there. I'll be back.' He opened the door of the bedroom and looked out into the corridor. There was no one there: by then the twins had let the mob into their room.

Seeing the door open across the way and hearing the chanting of revolutionary slogans from within, Pidduck crossed the corridor and entered the girls' room. In the weaving, chanting, banner-waving mass of figures in jeans, sweat shirts and smocks, the two German girls stood out in contrast since they still had no clothes on at all. They clung together, laughing stupidly. Pidduck pushed his way over to them.

'What's going on here?' he shouted in German.

152

'The General is in there,' Waldtraute shouted back, pointing to the bathroom, 'full of Coca-Cola.' She made a gesture depicting a protruding belly.

'What's so funny about Coca-Cola?' Pidduck demanded.

'Coca-Cola isn't funny, but he took it in at the wrong end,' Sieglinde shrieked. 'The wrong end, see?' and she made an indecent gesture.

Pidduck failed to grasp what they meant. 'What am I doing,' he asked himself, 'carrying on a meaningless conversation about Coca-Cola at the top of my voice with two naked, drunken tarts in the middle of a student riot, with an Indonesian General locked in the lavatory?'

Suddenly, the enormity of the situation dawned on him. 'Christ, the General's in there and probably stitchless too!' He looked around: draped over a chair in the corner were a man's clothes. He pushed his way into the crowd of milling students around the bathroom door. 'Who's the leader here?' he shouted. 'I want to talk to whoever's in charge of this mob.'

The chairman of the Marxist-Leninists came forward. He was carrying a banner proclaiming, *THE EMANCI-PATION OF THE OPPRESSED COLONIAL PEOPLES IS THE TASK OF THE PROLETARIAT AS A WHOLE – L. Trotsky*. He had been banging on the bathroom door with the pole. 'Greetings, Comrade,' he said to Pidduck. The din subsided as the demonstrators gathered round.

'Who the devil are you?' Pidduck asked.

The chairman explained.

'And what are you doing in these young ladies' room in the middle of the night?'

The chairman explained further. By now the place was quiet save for the moans from behind the bathroom door. Pidduck had an idea.

'Did you know,' he asked, 'that General Nasturtion has a serious heart condition?'

'We didn't,' the chairman said.

'Well, listen to him. If that man's not having a heart

attack right now, I'll eat my hat.'

They listened. The General sounded pathetic. 'He's locked himself in because he's scared of your mob,' Pidduck said. 'If you stay here and he's found dead on the floor it will mean second degree murder for the lot of you, at the very least. If you clear off now I'll see what I can do.'

'We have to present our demands,' the chairman said. 'It's what we're here for.'

'Give them to me. I'll present them.'

The Marxist-Leninists went into conference. 'It's petty bourgeois morality to feel compassion for the class enemy,' said a youth with red hair.

'We don't feel compassion,' the chairman said, 'but it's romantic adventurism to lay ourselves open to a murder rap and have our entire organization wiped out. Lenin taught one step back can lead to two steps forward. This would be our one step back.'

'But when will we take the two steps forward?' Marylou asked.

'It's a figure of speech, Marylou,' the chairman replied gently. 'It's meant to show that the revolutionary movement can't always advance. It has to retreat sometimes to regroup its forces. It needs historic perspective, right?'

A seminar was growing out of the riot: theory was being combined with practice. None of them seemed concerned either with the groaning General or the naked twins.

'Well, I'm a people person,' a girl in shorts said. 'I don't think we should make him die in the bathroom there. Some of you are into a whole destructive bag because you feel threatened.'

'That's crazy,' said the red-haired youth. 'You're unreal. Your thinking just isn't productive.'

'Oh, come on, get your head together,' the girl said.

'Hold it, hold it,' the chairman said. 'Why can't we stay with *politics*? First it's role models for women, then it's the behavioural psychology bit. Look, we've a *political* problem here and it needs a principled political response – a mature response . . .'

Pidduck intervened. 'I think you've discussed it enough. I think you should all clear off now so that I can get him out of there and send for a doctor.'

The chairman handed him a sheet of paper. 'Our demands are on there,' he said. 'See that the bastard gets them.'

'I will,' Pidduck said.

They trooped out in silence. At the door the taxi driver paused. 'I'm driving his taxi,' he said. 'I'll wait to take him back to the Guest House if he's well enough. Business is business.'

When he'd gone, Pidduck turned to the twins. 'Now,' he said, 'I want you to tell me what is wrong with the General.'

Waldtraute had sobered up enough to explain. 'God Almighty!' Pidduck said. 'I'm getting out of here. When he recovers, get him dressed and out to the taxi. Do you understand?

They said they did. George Pidduck returned to his room and the exhausting ministrations of Hildegarde. She didn't even ask what had been going on outside.

CHAPTER 14

Mr Sombolon in Room 53 lay awake listening to the distant sound of banging and shouting without connecting it in his mind with the General and the twins. He was thinking. Deeply and very carefully. He was thinking about the world economic situation and his personal affairs and finding an unmistakable link between them. He did not presume to an expert understanding of economics, but one thing he had felt reasonably sure about for some time: Britain as an economic power in the world was all washed up. On the skids. Dying but refusing to lie down and die decently. He didn't know what it was – she had lost her touch, her self-confidence. Something like that. She didn't seem able to perform, to out-smart the others any more. Mr Sombolon saw economic performance mainly in terms of manoeuvre, audacity and financial footwork. Having the mind of the middleman – being a textbook middleman himself – he was not much interested in production, product performance or industrial skills. It was a sphere of which he knew nothing. He judged All World by their ability to win contracts rather than their ability to perform on what they had won. Contract in hand, you could always talk yourself out of trouble. The performance side meant nothing to him: he assumed a bunch of grimy engineers would do what had to be done and he had nothing but disdain for what they did. His admiration was reserved for those who outsmarted the opposition and won the contract – for them and for the financial people who fixed payment terms, bank funding and the like. To Mr Sombolon the high water mark of British economic power and skill was Disraeli's purchase of the Suez Canal shares in 1875. Someone had told him of this greatest of politico-economic coups and he had understood it at once. He had also heard of what Rhodes had done in Africa and Raffles across the water in Singapore. All this showed brains, subtlety, an ability to fox the other side – to be last into the revolving doors and emerge first. But he had witnessed Britain's retreat from empire and was now witnessing her inability to hold onto her distant markets, and it was borne in upon him that he had tied his personal fortunes to those of a loser. Did not he himself, the representative of a British company, drive a Japanese car and listen to the stock market reports on a Japanese transistor? And the brand of after-shave he favoured had a French name but was owned by Americans. As he lay in bed in Room 53 of the Holiday Inn he decided solemnly and with a tinge of regret that self-interest dictated that he must do one thing: he must hedge his bets. True, All World was still in the race and going well. But it would be foolish to pretend that the Americans, and maybe the Japanese, coming up on the inside, could not get a nose in front in the last furlong, and here he was, the prudent and agile S.S. Sombolon, with all his money on the British. It was not wise. It was not even necessary. And so he decided that action was now required in defence of his personal interest. And having so decided, he turned on his side and slept.

Next morning he was up early. After bathing, dressing and saying his prayers, he paid a visit to Room 57 where he found Bill Watts with a powerful hangover and left him a half-hour later still feeling dreadful but, additionally astonished and greatly encouraged. Next he visited Room 71, where the Borkh twins were still in bed. Waldtraute let him in, a wrap covering a small part of her torso. In the space of five minutes he made it clear despite the language barrier that he had come for his two sums of $500 each, requested and promised back in Jakarta. The twins paid up, muttering to each other in German about thieving niggers. Then he called a taxi and paid a visit to General Nasturtion at the University Guest House.

If the General had been a European he would have looked yellow – possibly a deep enough yellow to have been taken for an Indonesian, such was his condition following his adventure of the night before. Being an Indonesian in the first place, the appalling state of his innards was not betrayed on his face, though an unwonted tentativeness in his manner – as if he were fragile and might break up on impact – signalled to Mr Sombolon that all was not right with him.

'I am deeply grieved to see you unwell,' he said.

'I had a terrible night,' the General said. He went on to explain what had happened, though he had no idea why – why his high colonic had left him in such agony, why a gang of hooligans had attacked the twins' room, or why they had suddenly departed. 'I believe,' he said, 'I was the target of vigilantes. Perhaps they were religious maniacs who objected on narrow grounds of so-called morality to my being with the Borkh twins. This is a terribly narrow-minded country.' He had had no time to read the slogans before retreating to the bathroom.

Mr Sombolon guessed at once what must have happened. 'You are certainly right,' he said. 'I am told they have many religious sects in the desert here who oppose licentiousness and enjoyment of all kinds. You must have had a most fortunate escape. You have my very deepest sympathy.' The General held his belly tenderly. It was still sore and internally disturbed. Also, he had a throbbing headache. 'Sombolon, I want you to make my excuses to the University President,' he said. 'I am not well enough for this tour this morning, nor for the formal lunch. In fact, I will not eat at all. If I rest I expect to be able to play my part in the ceremony this afternoon.'

'I will tell the President,' Mr Sombolon said.

'Good. And now, why did you come to see me?'

'I came, General, because all is not well,' Mr Sombolon said mysteriously.

'Explain yourself, Sombolon. Briefly, please. I am not

well enough for your lengthy preliminaries.'

'I appreciate your sad condition and am deeply grateful for your kindness and forbearance in . . .'

'Yes, yes, all right, Sombolon. Now come to the point.'

'I fear,' Mr Sombolon said portentously, 'a plot.'

'What kind of plot?'

Mr Sombolon now produced the ingenious theory he had thought up in the night: 'A plot by the Frenchmen,' he said, 'who cannot accept that your decision has gone against them.'

'That's crazy, Sombolon.'

'The French are very excitable people. I have heard it said that it is a nation of lunatics. At all events, I have information from a totally reliable source regarding this plot by the crazy Frenchmen.'

'So what is this plot?' The General winced as his large intestine appeared to knot itself within him. 'Hurry,' he said.

Mr Sombolon was unaware that the General's impatience was not on this occasion entirely temperamental. He therefore unravelled his complex and highly imaginative theory slowly and with loving care. Its ingenuity lay in this: the Americans must not be blamed since he now had designs on them himself, and the Japanese must also be officially blameless since he believed he could in the final analysis and if needs must, make some kind of deal with them. So who better than the French, who were already in the doghouse, to shoulder the blame for what might happen at the ceremony? And Mr Sombolon was now sure that something appalling would. 'My information,' he said carefully, 'is that the Frenchmen have mobilized the Japanese students at the University to create a disturbance at today's ceremony.'

'Good God,' the General said. 'It's utterly preposterous.'

'But the information, I am afraid, is good. There is no doubt about it. The Japanese are determined that you should lose face. The French have paid them to do it.'

159

'This is an outrage,' the General cried. 'How dare these Englishmen put me in such a position! I am surrounded by enemies and fools. What am I to do, Sombolon?'

'I am afraid my British associates have not been wise in this matter,' Mr Sombolon said. He shook his head sorrowfully. 'I personally feel that my loyalty must first of all be to you and that is why I am here now. I must also tell you that I am negotiating with the American student organizations to counter the Japanese plans and so enable the ceremony to take place. Alas, one can only counter force with force.'

The General looked like thunder. 'I will never deal with those swine again,' he said.

'The French?'

'The Japanese. Obviously, the French as well.'

'And the British?' Mr Sombolon's question was the merest ripple on the surface of the dialogue.

'We shall see,' General Nasturtion said. 'We shall see whether they have placed me in an impossible position.'

'I have taken the liberty of making contact with Galactic, the American company,' Mr Sombolon said, 'in case the other parties . . . fall out of the bidding. You may count on my complete cooperation and discretion, General, should you decide . . .' He trailed off, waving an expressive hand delicately before him. 'My allegiance,' he repeated, 'is to yourself. Always.'

'All right, Sombolon, we shall see. Now I must ask you to leave me.' His bowel was again in turmoil. 'At once,' he added.

Mr Sombolon rose, bowed and departed. He felt that his bets had been adequately hedged, providing the American had the right things to say to him after consulting his superiors at Fort Worth. He proceeded to the administration block to convey the General's message to Suzie. Then he phoned the Holiday Inn and asked for Room 57. What Bill Watts had to tell him was wholly satisfactory. Galactic would pay him a suitable commission should he demonstrate that his good offices

160

had resulted in their winning the Entakan contract.

The French and Japanese, he now considered, were out of the running. He, Sombolon, would be covered should the race go to the British – still favourites – or to the Americans, who could be considered as promising outsiders. No man could do more to guard against the twists and turns of a difficult fate and the fretfulness and unpredictability of General Nasturtion. It was not Mr Sombolon's fault that he knew nothing of the machinations of the Imperial Bank of Tokyo, nor of the left faction within the Japanese Students' Association at Hackberry and what they had done to broaden the base of the anti-Nasturtion campaign. Mr Sombolon had joined the growing ranks of those who imagined, wrongly, that they had some kind of grip on events.

The attendance at the ceremony was impressive: by two o'clock the open-air amphitheatre was packed with students and the stage was full of reluctant and complaining faculty members perspiring freely in their academic robes as they sat in the broiling sun awaiting the arrival of the principal performers. Meanwhile, the University's brass band was providing homely renderings of the lighter classics and items from the works of Souza and George Gershwin, followed by the overture to *Zampa* which the music critic on the campus newspaper was to subsequently call 'a spirited if injudicious rendering which did nothing for the reputation of the composer and substantial harm to that of the band'. The mood was cheerful in the main. The familiar odour of marijuana, burning slowly in countless joints, hung on the still air with no breeze to remove it. None of the furled banners, the placards on their poles, the baseball bats and other paraphernalia of insurrection was visible: they were tucked beneath the benches on which the students sat smoking, chewing gum, joshing, wisecracking and ripping the fasteners off cans of Coke, Sevenup, Pepsi, root beer, Schlitz and Budweiser.

But a careful observer might have noticed several

161

oddities: the complete absence of Japanese faces, for one thing; the presence of clusters of paunchy, hard-faced middle-aged men who looked out of place and ill at ease in this campus setting, for another; the very size of the audience at an event which could only prove to be deeply boring and would in normal circumstances have attracted virtually no one at all.

When at last President Harvey Zimmerman led the distinguished visitors onto the platform he was greeted with a good-natured Bronx cheer. The band, carefully but inadequately drilled, broke into a rendering of the Indonesian national anthem which left the audience unmoved in their seats since they had never heard it before, and left the General and the rest of the Indonesian party in much the same condition, though for the opposite reason: they had heard it repeatedly and this sounded nothing like it. They therefore sat down and remained seated until the band had finished on an unresolved suspension.

President Zimmerman had changed suits for the occasion and was perspiring freely, like the rest of the academics, in pale blue madras over which he wore the full regalia of his office. Suzie was delicious in shimmering white. The diamonds around the neck of General Nasturtion's wife glinted and flashed in the brilliant sunshine. The General himself was looking a little healthier, though beneath his black robe his stomach was still abominably sore and below his academic cap his complexion, to any other Indonesian, would appear unhealthily pale. He reckoned with luck to get through his speech and hopefully through the entire proceedings without having to rush from the platform. He had had no breakfast or lunch and felt as weak as a baby. But there was a hard and dangerous look in his eye. In its day that look had cost men of whom the General disapproved their lives. There was nothing babyish about it.

Seated further along the front row on the platform were George Pidduck, Nicos Papadopoulos, the Gener-

162

al's three children and at the far end of the line Mr Sombolon, relaxed like a man who reckoned he couldn't lose. In the space below the platform reserved for the press, four youthful reporters lounged listlessly, together with their Indonesian colleagues. One of them was from a leading news agency: someone had tipped them off that there would be trouble – with luck a decent little riot worth a couple of column inches to a number of their subscribers. The local radio station had sent a man and so had the campus newspaper. A small TV camera crew moved about, shooting footage at random with a hand-held camera and directional mike. 'Get the girl with the tits,' the man in charge would direct. 'Get the weirdo with the earrings. And the pregnant chick smoking the joint there. Did you *see* that?'

The man with the mike kept saying, 'Jesus, I'm picking up such crap here, there's nothing we could use.'

Near the press bench sat the Borkh twins, plump and identical in pink cheesecloth, exchanging heavy banter with their neighbours. They had been smoking for fifteen minutes and were high.

All this could be clearly seen. What remained invisible so far were the students' banners and placards and offensive weapons, the American Nazi Party and John Birch Society badges and offensive weaponry of the middle-aged spectators, and the body of over 100 Japanese, mustered behind the Humanities Block 200 yards away and ready to advance in close formation upon the amphitheatre. None of this was visible, but its imminence could be clearly felt by George Pidduck as he surveyed nervously the sea of milk-fed faces drawn up in neat lines before him and offered up a short but fervent prayer to a God he didn't believe in.

'Please, God, make it all right,' he muttered beneath his breath. 'Don't wreck it now we've come so far. After all, why should the Yanks get the contract? They don't need it as much as we do.'

He was aware that his non-existent deity had no sense of equity or justice – he'd had plenty of proof of it in the past – but in moments of crisis he couldn't resist making these useless little prayers. It was a habit from his childhood.

Praying even harder and with a good deal more conviction, Hildegarde Glauber lounged by the pool back at the Holiday Inn, dreaming of her Englishman and his problems, and their future together. 'Make him win!' she commanded her God. And in a more respectful tone, '*Please,* God, be kind to him for my sake and make the damn Americans lose. Amen!'

'Christ!' President Zimmerman was saying out of the corner of his mouth to Suzie, next to him on the platform, 'I don't like the look of this mob. Why the hell are they all here?'

'I don't know, honey,' Suzie said. 'Perhaps they're supporting this Third World thing, or something.'

'Third World my arse,' President Zimmerman snapped as the band recovered from the anthem and offered a brief rendering of *Yankee Doodle Dandy.* 'There's going to be trouble. I can smell it. The last time we had a crowd this size was to hear that shit-head O'Leary and that led to plenty trouble. No one's going to tell me these assholes want to hear this little yellow guy.'

'Shush, honey,' Suzie hissed at him. 'He'll hear you.'

'And all for two hundred grand,' Zimmerman said. 'Should be two-fifty and they robbed me of fifty. And now there's going to be big trouble. Come on, let's get the thing over with before they start shooting.'

He got to his feet as the band lapsed into silence, flicked the microphone to make sure it was live, and took a sheaf of notes from his pocket. As he held up a bejewelled hand for silence, the students produced an ironic cheer and a round of desultory clapping. Then an expectant hush fell on the packed amphitheatre and President Zimmerman cleared his throat.

'General Nasturtium, Sir, Madam Nasturtium, members of the faculty of this University, ladies and gentlemen . . .' His gravel voice rasped into the mike and was carried, booming, across the amphitheatre and out over the campus to be lost in the haze over towards the surrounding hills. 'Today is an historical occasion,' he snapped. 'It is my privilege and my pleasure, on behalf of my fellow-Americans, to welcome you, Sir, and your good lady to our shores, to this land of freedom and enterprise, and to the campus of our University here at Hackberry. You are here, General, so that we may bestow upon you an honour. That honour is the highest honour it is in our power to bestow . . .'

'I don't like this,' George Pidduck muttered to Papadopoulos next to him. 'I don't like it at all. No student body ever behaved like this unless they were up to something.' Papadopoulos nodded. 'And anyway, where are the Japanese? There isn't a single Jap in the place. They must be preparing some kind of attack. Oh, my God!'

'Steady, George,' Papadopoulos said, 'There's nothing you can do about it now so you might as well settle down to listen to this zombie. And take your head out of your hands; there's about a thousand people looking at you.'

President Zimmerman was getting into his stride. He had spent some time and care over his speech, aided by the highly fanciful material on General Nasturtion and Entakan supplied by Papadopoulos and a volume entitled *One Thousand Anecdotes for Public Speakers*. He was proud of what he had written, and if only he could overcome his sense of foreboding he would have been pleased to have such a large audience to listen to it. As he rasped into the microphone and the speakers carried his voice out across the campus, the audience listened respectfully.

The young man whose task it was to disconnect the mike was presently crawling about under the stage in search of the wires. As the President passed beyond the

165

dubious triumphs of General Nasturtion's military career and reached that part of his speech which dealt with the General's achievements at Entakan, leaders of opinion among the students began to wonder when the mike would go dead. It should do so any minute now, since the plan was that no one should hear anything of the General's subsequent remarks in reply.

'It is this man, this very great human being and representative of his ancient race,' President Zimmerman declaimed, 'that we are gathered here this afternoon to honour with the bestowment upon him of an honorary Doctorate at this, our great institution of learning. And it will now be my privilege and pleasure so to bestow that doctorate upon him in recognition of his outstanding contribution to the cause of . . .'

It was at this point that the young man came upon the wires and severed them with the cutters he had brought for the purpose. The rest of President Zimmerman's sentence was lost for ever. The sudden silence was the signal for which the Japanese students had been waiting. With cries of *Banzai!* they set out at a steady trot, eight abreast, towards the amphitheatre. They wore sweatbands round their heads and their leader, like any guide at Tokyo airport, bore aloft a red flag inscribed with Japanese characters. Their arms were linked. It was a formidable and frightening force, and as they drew nearer to their goal they quickened their pace to a run and yelled their slogans in an angry crescendo of sound which reached the audience ahead of them.

'That's the Japs,' Pidduck said despairingly. 'We're done for.'

A general murmuring had started in the audience and among the faculty members on the platform. But determined to complete the ceremony and collect his money, President Zimmerman soldiered on with his speech, cutting out sizeable chunks in order to reach the formal presentation ahead of the disaster he now felt to be looming over the proceedings. Nothing he said could

166

be heard.

The distant murmur of voices was growing on the wind and was now clearly audible as an angry, alien-sounding roar. President Zimmerman struggled to make himself heard above the increasing hubbub.

'I therefore have much pleasure,' he yelled hoarsely, 'on behalf of this University, in bestowing upon you, General, the honorary title of Doctor of Philosophy.' As he shouted the words he turned towards the General's seat next to him, beribboned scroll in hand. But the General was no longer there. Provoked no doubt by the mounting excitement, his rebellious gut had once again had its way with him and he had staggered away to the toilets behind the stage, clutching his belly and moaning quietly. To the students his disappearance needed no explanation: he was scared. It was the signal for action.

Suddenly the whole amphitheatre burst into a multi-coloured rash of waving banners, streamers and placards, while a confused roar of slogans and counter-slogans rose up and engulfed the stage. At this moment, two other things also happened. To cries of 'Get the Commie bastards!' and 'Keep America white!', the American Nazi Party and their allies formed into a phalanx, drew their coshes and truncheons, and advanced down the central aisle, flailing at the students to their left and right, while behind them the 100-odd Japanese, whipped into a self-induced lather of militant self-sacrifice, entered the arena at a gallop and, unable to stop, ran in a solid, heaving mass down the same aisle in pursuit, as it were, of the Nazis.

The first victims of the Nazi attack proved to be the ecology group. Preferring to sit on the ground in the lotus position, they had shifted from their benches into the aisle, where they sat crosslegged in their loose flowing garments, chewing a few nuts and drinking milk obtained from an approved herd. Their banners dealt exclusively with whales, seals, obscure sea birds and the need for biodegradable packaging. They were chanting in unison a slogan on the theme of hydrocarbon resources. None of it could be heard in the confused uproar which now prevailed. The yelling Nazis trampled over the ecologists, toppling them and tearing their placards to shreds. Not believing in violence and having no offensive weapons, the ecologists offered no resistance. Greatly encouraged, the Nazis advanced down the aisle.

Meanwhile, the brass band, safely off to the side of the stage and possibly aware that the combo aboard the *Titanic* had played foxtrots as the ship went down, broke into a pot-pourri from *The Student Prince*.

And now the Marxist-Leninists, principled, disciplined and ideologically united for once, formed up over to the left and at a signal from their chairman, rushed the platform. A youth bearing a banner proclaiming 'WHAT HAPPENED TO THOSE WHALES, GENERAL?' was knocked senseless in the rush and his banner trampled underfoot. Another with a placard demanding 'LEGALIZE HASH' met much the same fate. A girl with the message 'VIOLENCE IS A MALE INVENTION' was sent flying by a 280-pound Nazi. 'Truest thing you ever said, you lousy red bitch,' he roared at her as she lay between the benches. Nearby the Borkh twins were pummelling into insensibility a diminutive Japanese student of economics who had got ahead of his compatriots and had so far misjudged matters as to scream at them in his native tongue. '*Schweinhund!*' yelled Sieglinde. '*Dumkopf!*' cried Waldtraute. A Japanese contingent descended on the twins and snatched their battered comrade from beneath them. In the ensuring fracas their cheesecloth was largely ripped away and a cheer went up in their immediate vicinity. Once again the twins were largely naked.

'Come on, comrades, show the imperialist swine the workers say "No",' cried the taxi driver from the front of the Marxist-Leninist task force. A nearby Nazi from Phoenix felled him with a blow to the back of the head from a wooden mallet. Diverted from their objective by this incident, the Marxist-Leninists turned towards the

Nazis and John Birchers. A savage battle was fought beneath the platform as the members of the press scrambled for safety. The TV crew moved in to get a tight shot of the rough stuff and within moments $50,000 worth of electronic news-gathering equipment lay in pieces on the ground.

By now the battle was general, much of it conducted erroneously between allies. The powerful black men from Zanzibar, confused by the events of the past minutes, concluded that the Nazis were probably the good guys and fought shoulder to shoulder with them. They were puzzled by the absence of Indians.

'Get the General!' yelled the chairman of the Marxist-Leninists. 'Don't forget the class enemy, Comrades. Don't be diverted from the main task!' A group under his leadership made their way to the back of the stage and once again the General was besieged in the lavatory.

'Why is it,' he asked himself grimly, 'that whenever I try to take a crap in this place I am attacked by a mob of lunatics?'

Back on the platform, President Zimmerman had given up all attempt to control the meeting. As soon as the horde of Japanese appeared at the back of the amphitheatre he had sent Suzie to phone for the police. 'Tell 'em we've a riot on our hands and they'd better alert the Governor,' he said. 'We'll probably need the National Guard. Tell 'em we've a foreign VIP here and it's shaping into a diplomatic incident. Tell 'em it looks like being worse than last time.'

Then he pushed his way over to Nicos Papadopoulos. 'I made the award,' he yelled over the hubbub. 'You heard me do it. Just in time. The guy's a Ph.D. so you owe me 250 grand and I want it now.'

'What's that? I can't hear you,' Papadopoulos answered, though he could hear him perfectly well.

'Two-fifty you owe me. I want it – now.' The President was hoarse from shouting.

'When this is over,' Papadopoulos cried. 'We'll go to

169

the bank together.' He was not anxious to discuss money in front of George Pidduck.

'All right, but I want it settled this afternoon.'

'I understand.'

The Japanese advance guard had now overrun the press table, scattering the astonished Indonesian journalists who were trying to take notes and wondering if they would dare file their stories. The most ambitious of them had already scribbed out a lead which he judged would make page one of his paper:

'The overwhelming enthusiasm of American students for solidarity with the Indonesian people, nobly represented by General Nasturtion of Entakan, led to an unfortunate riot here today as the young people struggled to see and perhaps to shake the hand of our great man . . .'

It was snatched out of his hand and trampled underfoot by the attacking Japanese.

Now fierce oriental faces surmounted by red headbands began to appear at floor level on the edge of the platform, quickly to be hoisted up by their fellow-combatants. In no time the Japanese were among the platform party. They had worked themselves into a lather of national feeling and anti-imperialist passion. They screamed unintelligible slogans and waved banners inscribed with sweeping demands in Japanese. They shook their fists beneath the noses of startled Professors of Ancient Greek and English Literature. They yelled '*Banzai!*' and stamped in unison. And while they were thus making their opinions manifest, the Nazis were clambering onto the platform in turn.

'C'mon, get the yellow scum!' shouted their leader, brandishing a useful-looking nightstick borrowed from his regular job as a policeman. 'Get the little bastards! Kill the motherfuckers.' He lunged at the nearest Japanese. Missing his target he fetched the President a nasty jab in the groin, doubling him up and attracting a spluttering tirade in language that he could understand.

170

'We don't take that from a fucking Jewboy,' he cried, and brought the nightstick down on the President's skull, felling him in an untidy heap on the floor. The leader of the Nazis then returned to the Japanese, who might be smaller but were far more numerous and agile. To the sound of yells, grunts, splintering chairs and falling bodies, the battle engulfed the stage and its occupants, punctuated by shrill screams of indignation and whispers of distress from the more elderly lady lecturers. Pidduck, Papadopoulos, Mr Sombolon and others retreated to the comparative safety of the space behind the platform, leading Harvey Zimmerman, who was in no fit condition to find his own way. Sounds of banging, punctuated by cries of 'Freedom to the peasant masses!' came from the direction of the toilets.

'Oh, God,' George Pidduck moaned, 'they've caught him in the bog again. Come on, we'll have to get him out of there.'

Papadopoulos and Mr Sombolon followed him. And it was at this point that in answer to Suzie's tearful pleas on the telephone a police siren made itself heard above the roar of battle. The cry went up: 'Get the pigs!' There was a movement towards the exit by the more excitable students. As they emerged from the amphitheatre the wail of the siren died away. Facing the advance guard of students out for blood stood a solitary patrolman by his motorbike. He had been summoned by radio to take a look at the situation on the campus and now he stood, resplendent in leather, crash helmet, dark glasses, gun belt and gauntlets by the side of his Harley Davidson from which instructions, queries and call signs crackled into the hot afternoon. He stood legs apart and arms akimbo, the personification of law and order and terrified out of his wits. He surveyed the yelling mob, growing rapidly and advancing towards him across a hundred yards of well irrigated turf. Then he did the sensible thing. He turned his bike and roared off towards the safety of the highway, where he radioed a full-scale riot to HQ.

171

'Where are you?' they asked him.

'On Highway 288 between Hackberry and Falls Valley, travelling west.'

'Why ain't you on campus?'

'There's a fucking insurrection goin' on up there. It's a job for the Guard.'

'Aw, let 'em kill each other. Over and out.'

Having routed the Arizona Police Department, the more militant souls among the students turned back to the amphitheatre to seek new enemies. There were only the Nazis and their friends available, but grossly outnumbered as they were, there was no room for anyone else to get at them. The Japanese, diverted from their original quarry, were now swarming all over the overweight Nazis like ants attacking and defeating much larger creatures by sheer numbers. As one Japanese was flung aside by a burly Nazi, three others leapt upon him. Garments were torn, heads bloodied, shins cracked and glasses in great numbers smashed to the ground. It was a great day for the optometrists. Slowly the Nazis retreated, dragging their wounded and throwing aside their weapons like any defeated army abandoning the field. The Japanese harassed and tormented them as they took to their heels and headed for the car park and their coaches. It was a famous victory, and cheers echoed across the campus as the retreat was finally concluded.

The proceedings had now lost all cohesion and unity of purpose as the various student groups reverted to their sectional interests. The ecology group had gathered and tended their wounded and were now regaining their peace of mind by passing round a few joints and listening to a little country and western on a transistor. Much the same thing was happening among the mystically-oriented students. They had lost what little interest they had had in General Nasturtion and were indifferent to the skirmishes taking place around them. A certain amount of harmless praying was going on, much of it to oriental gods.

The group from Zanzibar, mystified by almost every-thing that had happened that afternoon, had assembled in a small circle and were singing something repetitive and seemingly endless from their native land. They had abandoned all hope of locating and assaulting any Indian traders. Their song spoke, in their obscure dialect, largely of cattle, and its binary musical form had distinct modal leanings though they didn't know it:

> *Abu's cow is in calf,*
> *Hola, hola!*
> *Whose cow?*
> *Abu's cow,*
> *Ho, ho!*

This was repeated a number of times for emphasis.

A group of young men who had managed skilfully to stay out of the fighting were putting the finishing touches with needle and thread to a banner which proclaimed in patchwork WHY NO GAYS ON THE BOARD OF REGENTS?

Back in the men's toilets, the Marxist-Leninists had once again been deflected from action in order to engage in theoretical debate.

'Why don't you stop persecuting General Nasturtion?' George Pidduck demanded. 'What has the man ever done to you?'

'He represents imperialist exploitation and its lackeys in the Third World, and the rape of the world's natural resources,' the chairman of the Marxist-Leninists replied. 'In attacking him as a symbol of reaction we are making a political statement that the broad masses will understand.'

'But the broad masses don't know what's going on here in the men's room.'

'We didn't plan our protest to take place in the can, for God's sake,' the chairman said. 'We're only here because the General hid himself in here. It's where he always ends up.'

'What would Comrade Bukharin have done?' an

173

emaciated girl demanded. 'He opposed Lenin on the democratic issue. He demanded discussion by the masses. We should take the issue to the people.'

'Try not to talk doctrinaire nonsense, Melanie,' the chairman said. 'You want we should call a mass meeting to debate the question: Do we go after the General in the can? The issue isn't ripe for public debate, Comrade. I've warned you before about your leftist tendencies. They lead to counter-revolutionary populism, Melanie. They objectively serve the interests of the class enemy, right?'

'Right,' said Melanie, crestfallen.

'Remember what happened to Zinoviev,' the chairmen said darkly.

'We're taking two steps forward in the revolutionary struggle,' Marylou said from the back of the crowd. 'I guess we're making this whole bit about the General's Ph.D. an issue of principle. It's an affront to the working people of the world and particularly to the exploited peasant masses of Indonesia. That's why our two steps . . .'

'Yes, Marylou,' the chairman said, 'we see that. But right now we have a practical problem of revolutionary tactics: do we break down the door of the can or do we not?'

There were shouts of, 'Let's go get him!' and counter-cries of, 'Leave him in there. Let's have a sit-in at Zimmerman's office!'

'Quiet, comrades,' shouted the chairman. 'We'll take a vote on leaving the General where he is or going in after him.'

A show of hands found in favour of the General being left to emerge in his own time and the Marxist-Leninists moved off to debate the next move in the struggle.

'That zombie Zimmerman is making all kinds of threats. I'd better take him off to the bank,' Papadopoulos said to George Pidduck. 'I checked and the funds are through, so it should only take the time to get to Hackberry and back.'

'All right,' Pidduck said, 'I'll look after the General. He's likely to come out of there shooting from both hips.'

At that moment Suzie appeared. 'There's a message on the fax for the General,' she said. 'It asks him to go straight back to Jakarta tomorrow.'

'I'll give it to him,' Pidduck told her. 'He won't be pleased. Oh, my God!'

A little later that afternoon the transaction involving $250,000 between Nicos Papadopoulos and President Harvey Zimmerman at the First Farmers' Bank of Hackberry was duly completed, with $50,000 in cash changing hands afterwards in the President's car. 'For the flaming pussycats and geriatrics,' the President said sourly as he counted out the last of the bills and handed them over.

There had been a nasty moment when the bank officer had said to Papadopoulos 'Do you have any instructions for us on the further sum transferred from Barclays, Singapore?'

This was the further $50,000 Papadopoulos had told George Pidduck would have to be paid to Zimmerman as a sweetener but which was destined for his own pocket. Zimmerman pricked up his ears but Papadopoulos was quick to lower the pressure. 'No, that's a personal transaction of mine,' he told the bank teller. 'I'll phone my instructions through to you.'

Harvey Zimmerman had thought for a moment that there might be more where the $250,000 came from.

As they passed the Holiday Inn on the way back to the campus neither of them noticed a disconsolate figure standing on the porch and gazing without hope along the road into the dusty distance. It was Bill Watts, certain that the Galactic plan had been defeated since the riot had turned out to be overwhelmingly an American party, and equally certain that he would go down in the annals of Galactic as the briefest occupant in the company's history of the post of Vice-president for Sales. Unless, he reflected without much conviction, the furtive little Indonesian who had visited him in his room that morning could salvage something from the afternoon's disaster, though he couldn't see what or how. The Japanese must have ignored his instructions after all and told the rest of the students. It was that girl: she'd made it obvious she didn't think much of his plan.

But what could he have done to prevent it? Nothing. And would the President of Galactic recognize as much? No, he would not. For him, as Bill Watts knew very well from countless staff meetings, brainstormers, think-ins, seminars and Memos from the Office of the President, excellence was the name of the game. You had to achieve excellence in all you did for the company. And to achieve it you required one thing above all: leverage. Those currently were the magical buzz words of American business and the President of Galactic had seized on them like a man desperate for certainties, and made them his own. And now one thing was clear beyond a peradventure to Bill Watts as he turned back to the lobby, heading for the solace of the bar: he had lacked leverage with the Japanese, and whatever he had achieved at the University, it wasn't excellence. But maybe the Indonesian with the furtive manner could help after all . . .

CHAPTER
15

Later that fateful Monday, explanations were the order of the day – explanations, recriminations, evasions and grovelling apologies. Since the plans of everyone with the shining exception of Nicos Papadopoulos had gone hopelessly awry, it was not surprising.

There was also a simple question posed and awaiting a reply: with everyone's copybook now blotted beyond hope of cleaning, what would the General do? To whom would that unpredictable and bloody-minded little despot award the contract?

True, the British had procured him his coveted Ph.D. and had a substantial track record of compliant venality, including the provision of massive German tarts. But the British had also exposed him to unspeakable loss of face and humiliation and what should have been a PR triumph had turned into a miserable farce.

The action of the Japanese students had confirmed all his deep-seated anti-Japanese prejudices. Their behaviour had proved yet again that no good could ever come of allowing the Communists to participate in a country's political life. If the Japanese Government had any sense they would shoot the lot of them, as General Nasturtion and his colleagues had done in Indonesia. And like the Japanese, the American students had confirmed the jaundiced view that he had held of the United States ever since they had decided to call it a day in Vietnam.

And the French, if Mr Sombolon were to be believed, had sinned horribly and had sinned twice. It left no one with clean hands.

So the General could be expected to choose almost at random among the protagonists, according to the whim of the moment, since all of them were willing to bribe him to the requisite extent. And since the British had, with their Ph.D., already done it, there were some grounds for supposing that they still had a slight but useful edge. They certainly had a moral claim to the contract. But there again the General wasn't one to give much weight to moral considerations: he had never heard of them.

'I will make my decision back in Jakarta,' he told Mr Sombolon, who had summoned up the courage to ask him. 'I shall leave this disgusting place in the morning and return via New York and Paris. I have been asked to fly straight home but that is not convenient to my wife, who has more shopping to do. Send the Borkh twins straight back to Jakarta. Bringing them to Paris would be too complicated.'

'Certainly, General. And is there any other way I can be of service?'

'You can travel with us. It might be of use to me.'

'Very good, General. It will be my pleasure to make the arrangements.' Mr Sombolon was pleased to be able to keep the General under observation. One never knew who would try to get at him in New York or Paris. Furthermore, it would be possible to draw some useful expenses from George Pidduck.

Under the crisp headline RIOT MARS GEN'S AWARD, the wire service had put out some ten paragraphs containing four errors of fact and two fairly basic misunderstandings. But they had got it right that Entakan was in oil (though they had misspelt their name) and this led a number of Texan papers to print truncated versions of the story, in which further violence was done to the facts. As it finally reached the breakfast table of Galactic's President, the General had been severely beaten by American Communists and other left subversives and had been hospitalized after the sheriff's men had saved him from a lynching.

Reading this, the President choked on his cereal,

refused his yoghurt, and stamped out to his car without kissing anyone. At the office he ordered the immediate recall of Bill Watts.

'I might have known it,' he shouted. 'A man with a background like that! A lousy pinko! Get the stupid little prick back here – fast. And get his name off that office door. And I want to know who let him into the company.'

With Bill Watts heading for his fate in Fort Worth and the Borkh twins and Hildegarde flying westwards across the Pacific towards Jakarta, the General's party with Mr Sombolon in attendance was flying east to Paris, Dior and Cartier. George Pidduck decided he could take in London on his way back to Jakarta for what he hoped would be the triumphal finale. He arrived in time for the quarterly meeting of the full Board of Directors of All World Oil Services.

'You can report progress on this Indonesian shambles of yours,' Rufus Pipe told him. 'But for Christ's sake be careful what you say. Don't forget the outside directors. You'll be talking to a gaggle of washerwomen. They even gossip to taxi drivers.'

'I know,' Pidduck said. 'They're like babies with candy: can't be trusted with it.'

'Be careful of old Lord Stowmarket,' Pipe said. 'He's very touchy these days. Fast sinking into a kind of senile idiocy and often nasty with it.'

Pidduck nodded agreement. 'Always gets hold of the wrong end of the stick.'

'About time they had him seen to.'

'Or put down.'

In Pipe's outer office Pidduck was reunited with the nubile and enthusiastic Daphne.

'Missed you lots, my sweet,' she said.

'I missed you too. How are you fixed tonight?'

'I kept it for you.' She seemed to refer both to the evening and the relevant parts of her anatomy.

At the board meeting on the following afternoon, George Pidduck's report on the negotiations for the

Entakan servicing contract, cleaned-up and sanitized, would not have raised so much as an eyebrow in the office of the Director of Public Prosecutions. Lord Stowmarket and another director were asleep at the time, but those who were awake nodded approvingly.

'What Mr Pidduck has had to tell us,' said an outside director whose presence on the board was a mystery dating back to the early post-war years, 'is a very fine tribute to British craftsmanship and his own abilities as a negotiator. I congratulate him. I often tell my friends in the City that this country can still beat the Japanese and Americans by an innings. Beat 'em on quality, eh, eh? British quality, eh? Is that not so, Mr Pidduck, eh, eh?'

'Yes, yes,' George Pidduck said, answering both interrogatives and marvelling at the witless innocence of the man. 'Indeed, yes. Quite.'

It was at that point that Lord Stowmarket stirred uneasily and awoke. He muttered incoherently for a while, glanced round the table in some astonishment at being where he was, and announced: 'I see that our friend Andrew Macready is asleep. Is that in order, Chairman?'

'Perhaps not,' the Chairman said, 'but let's get on with the meeting, shall we?'

'But Macready's asleep,' Lord Stowmarket insisted. He turned to the slumbering Macready, whose breathing was on the stertorous side but not such as to disrupt the proceedings. 'Wake up!' he yelled suddenly. 'This is the Bench, you know, not the smoking room of the club. Wake up, man!'

Startled, the unfortunate Macready jerked awake, sending his half-full coffee cup flying across the boardroom table. 'Er, er, I say, very sorry, Chairman.' He mopped at the spilled coffee with his papers.

'Clumsy fool,' Lord Stowmarket said in a stage whisper. 'Sleeps on the Bench and then flings the tea things all over the place. And they want solicitors to plead in the High Court, someone said. Next case!'

180

The Chairman coughed, and decided to play it for laughs. 'Hah!' he exclaimed. 'Ha, ha! Very good, Humphrey. Next case, quite. The next case, as you put it, is the review of the quarterly figures, but we haven't quite finished yet with George Pidduck's report on the, er, the Entakan thing, is it George?'

'Yes, Chairman.'

'What on earth are you talking about?' demanded his Lordship, still under the impression that he was on the Magistrate's Bench. '*What's the man saying?*' he yelled in Macready's ear.

'It's the All World board, Humphrey,' Macready whispered. 'Not the Bench. The board.' But the news did not reach Lord Stowmarket, who had already fallen back into a troubled sleep.

'Let us proceed,' the Chairman sighed, wondering how they could drop Lord Stowmarket at the next AGM without inheriting an even more unsatisfactory representative of the Stowmarket family interests. There was said to be a son who, had he hailed from a less august clan, would long since have been certified, and another who was big in the drugs trade out of Colombia. Senile and disputatious the old boy might be, but he was at least harmless and not, as far as was known, wanted by the police of two continents. Perhaps, the Chairman pondered ruefully, he should be allowed to sink into final decay and dissolution where he was.

'I would like to know,' said the outside director who admired British quality, 'what it is precisely that has swung this important contract our way.'

'Past performance and nothing else,' Rufus Pipe said crisply.

'We haven't got the contract yet, you know,' Pidduck said. 'It's looking good but we still need a signature.'

'Good, good,' the outside director said, amid dark mutterings from the sleeping Stowmarket. 'But I think I should mention, Chairman, that there's talk in the City of a bit of a crisis at Entakan. They defaulted this month, you know.'

181

'I know. But our bankers assure us the Indonesian Government will bail them out. It's the view of the Foreign Office, too.'

'I also heard there's a move afoot to replace their chairman. Some General. Can't recall the blighter's name. It appears the Japs are pressing for it.'

'*What?*' George Pidduck yelped. 'How hard is that?'

'It's what I heard in the City, that's all,' the outside director said. 'Does it affect us?'

'Affect us? Why, it could finish us,' Pidduck said.

'But if it's on British quality –' the outside director began.

'Good thing you're getting back to Jakarta, isn't it?' Rufus Pipe put in hastily. 'George here will be leaving tonight, Chairman, so I suggest we leave things as they are until we hear from him.'

'A hundred pounds or three months,' Lord Stowmarket announced. 'Next case.' He peered at the Chairman, mistaking him for some unsavoury felon. Then he resumed his nap, while the meeting meandered to an uncertain close.

That evening George Pidduck again caught the Singapore Airlines flight eastwards after telling Mr Sombolon on the phone to Paris to abandon the Nasturtion party and follow him to Jakarta at once.

The same evening, at the Ritz in Paris, Mr Sombolon caught sight of a portly, morning-suited personage in the lobby who seemed to exercise wide authority in the place.

'Please, who is that gentleman?' he asked the concierge.

'That is our General Manager,' he was told.

Mr Sombolon was well pleased with this information. 'Kindly tell him,' he said, 'that my esteemed friend General Nasturtion will have much appreciations of personal visit from your General Manager. General Nasturtion is very big man in our country, isn't it. You will tell this to your General Manager.'

182

'Very good, Monsieur.'

He told the General later, 'I understand the manager of the hotel will be presenting his compliments, I saw him in the lobby today. He must be a very good manager.'

'Why do you say that, Sombolon?'

'Because,' Mr Sombolon said, his eyes averted and his posture signalling devotion, 'he has been awarded the popular French decoration you once asked me about, the Legion of Honour. You will observe the little red rosette in his buttonhole. I did not know they gave it to managers of hotels.'

Mr Sombolon was taking no chances on a renewal of pro-French sentiment on the General's part.

George Pidduck, the General's family, Mr Sombolon, Hildegarde and the Borkh twins all arrived back in Jakarta within a couple of days of each other. It was as if the show, having played Hackberry, Arizona, had now moved back to Jakarta for a final performance. All, or nearly all, the players had now assembled. The Japanese had quietly returned from Tokyo. Harold Foreman of Galactic was still there, wondering if Fort Worth had forgotten him, which they had. Only the defeated French were absent. And, of course, the General. He had booked his return flight on the French UTA airline two days later. It was UT566 via Singapore. He did not regard it as sound tactics to respond to any kind of demand from the Prime Minister.

UT566 flew into the airspace controlled by Dubai International Airport at 2025 hours and made radio contact with the control tower. At 2048 it first appeared on the controller's radar screen and the pilot was instructed to descend to 1500 metres in a holding pattern. The runway would be busy for the next fifteen minutes: congestion caused by a couple of late arrivals from the East. The UTA pilot did what he was told after cursing briefly in French, but the pilot of an executive jet flying in from Beirut did not.

The mid-air collision clipped half the port wing off the UTA Boeing, which plummeted onto the foreshore. There were no survivors.

CHAPTER 16

The Armenian funeral contractor whose services were retained by Entakan to bring the remains of their late chairman back to Jakarta was a man of infinite resource and sound business acumen, but in this instance his professional ingenuity was strained to the limit. For in the case of General Nasturtion, deceased, he was confronted with a puzzling task.

When a large aircraft crashes, the bodies of the occupants are liable to be neither in one piece nor the pieces in one place, and the Dubai crash was no exception. The plane's tanks had exploded, distributing fragmented corpses far and wide. The rescue services had done what they could, but they had perforce ended up with a fairly heterogeneous collection of human remains and this shambles had put a considerable strain on the limited resources of the local morgue. In Dubai's steaming summer climate, early disposal became an urgent necessity. Thus, by the time the Armenian contractor reached the scene from Bahrain, there was little enough in the way of corpses to choose from and none of them recognizable.

Determined not to have his valuable contract declared null and void, the Armenian had made a selection more or less at random among the human debris and having assembled some 120 lbs of likely-looking segments, had packed them into an expensive coffin which he had brought in by air from New York. Then he saw it safely into the cargo hold of a Garuda chartered aircraft, sent out specially by Entakan.

What in fact he was despatching to Jakarta were portions of the last earthly remains of a French construction engineer and an elderly Pakistani textile exporter. There was also a small and not very significant part of an Indian lady from Hyderabad. Much depended on the Indonesians not opening the coffin on arrival, and the contractor telexed firmly on this point: any sight of the General's remains would cause extreme distress to the observer and particularly to his relatives. For this reason, he explained in his telex, he had soldered the lid of the coffin's metal lining and had screwed down the walnut top after making a liberal application of adhesive at the edges. A crowbar and blowlamp would be needed to get the thing open.

In the event, his luck held and the Frenchman, the Pakistani and the lady from Hyderabad were to be partly disposed of in accordance with the rituals of the Muslim faith. The Jakarta press, venal as ever and terrified of the General even in death, heaped fulsome praises upon him and shed tears of unquenchable sorrow. They ran very large pictures of the coffin provided by the Armenian contractor, and told their readers in all innocence that it enclosed the General's remains. A memorial service, they announced, would be attended by the Prime Minister and his Government colleagues, whose grief at the passing of the great man knew no bounds.

The Prime Minister, whose relief it was that was unbounded, discussed the new situation with his Minister of Mines. 'It solves our little problem with the Japanese,' he said.

'It does.'

'And I suppose it will mean the end of the risk that . . .' He searched for a phrase of suitable delicacy, '. . . that this material he is said to hold will prove damaging to us . . . the files secreted in Geneva?'

'I hope so,' the Minister of Mines said. 'I sincerely hope so.'

'Tell me,' the Prime Minister said, dropping his voice and leaning towards his colleague, 'did you, er, arrange this thing, eh?'

'Definitely not,' the Minister said. 'It undoubtedly was

the will of Allah. I had no resources at my disposal to cause the crash.'

'Whereas,' the Prime Minister said, 'Allah the Great One has.'

They smiled.

'You will attend the ceremony?' the Minister asked.

'Most certainly, and I shall be seen to weep. And so will you.'

'And who will succeed him?'

'I am thinking about that. I will have to consult the President. He may want it for one of his idiot nephews. Also, the Japanese ambassador is seeing me later today. No doubt he will have his nominee. If it proves to be you, my friend, I will know who paid for your wife's emeralds.'

But the Japanese ambassador's instructions had been drafted with subtlety. 'We would respectfully request knowledge of your nominee for the chairmanship of Entakan,' he said, 'before publication of same,' he murmured, 'and if it is convenient to your Excellency.' He smiled unconvincingly into his tea. 'We would not be altogether happy, of course, with a chairman of known anti-Japanese sentiments. And your Excellency will appreciate that it would add greatly to international banking confidence if the new chairman were to be a man of proven financial capacity – perhaps a cautious and conservative person from the banking field whose policy would be one of retrenchment and financial orthodoxy.'

'Quite, Mr Ambassador,' the Prime Minister said. 'Do you have anyone in view?'

'I would never presume . . .' The ambassador smiled again, leaving the thought in mid-air. 'But my Government would deem it a mark of cordial relations between our countries if they could be advised in advance.'

'Of course,' the Prime Minister said, choking back his indignation at this crass interference in Indonesian internal affairs. He rose, indicating that the interview was at an end.

'The one thing we have to avoid,' he told the Minister of Mines afterwards, 'is putting in someone who is in the pockets of those damnable people. But how shall we know?'

'There is no way to know,' the Minister said philosophically. 'Put in the best man and hope the Americans will offer him more.'

'You are very cynical, my friend.'

'I have lived for fifty-three years. I have had time to learn.'

'Would you take the job?'

'Why should I wish to acquire the largest headache in Asia?'

'Then I would like a list of candidates from you by tomorrow.'

The funeral and memorial ceremony for General Nasturtion took place in Jakarta in an atmosphere of solemn piety and maudlin but spurious grief such as can only be generated when it is felt necessary to mark the departure of a well-hated man. Everyone whose self-interest dictated that they should be present was in attendance. Perhaps the only mourners feeling truly sorry at the General's demise were those who stood to lose by it: the German girls, whose assignment in Jakarta had been, after all, relatively painless as such assignments went, and George Pidduck, who had just spent a small fortune to no purpose whatever.

'How do you view this new situation?' Dr Pak Sombolon asked his brother as they sat side by side, eyeing the splendid American coffin on its catafalque.

'I would prefer that he had lived until the signing of the contract,' his brother said. 'And no longer,' he added.

'Who will replace him?'

'I do not know, but there is talk of his deputy. Also of General Ruino, who is related to the President. They also mention the Minister of Mines. In all these cases I have possibilities.'

'I suppose,' Dr Sombolon said ruefully, 'the German ladies will be sent home.'

'I suppose so.'

'A pity. I have rarely seen such . . .'

'Yes,' his brother said, 'you always liked these fleshy northern women. Fleshy and pale, as if the light never reaches them. A strange taste.'

Dr Sombolon sought a change of subject, 'I see that your Armenian friend has supplied a fine coffin.' He knew his sexual tastes were viewed with much contempt in the family and didn't wish to discuss the matter further.

Mr Sombolon it had been, resourceful and helpful as ever, who had put Entakan in touch with the Armenian funeral contractor after negotiating a commission with the latter. It was to him that the Armenian had telephoned in dismay and panic from Dubai.

'I cannot identify the body,' he had complained bitterly.

'Does it matter?' Mr Sombolon asked simply.

The Armenian had a quick mind. 'You mean . . .' he said.

'That is right, my friend.' Mr Sombolon saw no need to state the obvious and did not trust the telephone. 'Will they let you take what you need?'

'I do not see how it can be missed. Who would miss a slice of orange from a fruit salad?'

Mr Sombolon grimaced slightly into the telephone. 'Solder the lid,' he said.

'I understand.'

'And my commission is now thirty per cent.'

'That is an outrage,' the Armenian shouted.

'Soldered it is thirty. Unsoldered, twenty.'

'I will lose money.'

'Then give up the contract. No man should be asked to lose on a contract.'

'My professional reputation demands that I fulfil my obligations.'

'Thirty per cent.'

189

'Twenty-five.'

'Twenty-seven and a half.'

'Agreed.'

And there rested the carved walnut coffin before them, with its heavy brass handles and dubious contents.

In the section reserved for the Diplomatic Corps sat the French and Japanese ambassadors, side by side. The French ambassador felt that he represented in a sense those who had inadvertently killed the General, while the Japanese felt that he was there on behalf of those who rejoiced in the fact. He sought to transmit carefully to his French colleague a discreetly worded expression of solidarity. This he conveyed with such subtlety that the Frenchman failed utterly to grasp the point and imagined he was referring to the recent action of the consortium of Entakan's creditor banks, in which the French had been among the hawks.

'We had to do it,' the French ambassador said. 'The situation was, in our view, becoming untenable. Our people do not like doing that kind of thing, of course, and they only acted after the Quai d'Orsay and the *Finances* had given their consent.'

'A delicate matter,' the Japanese said. '*Entre collègues,* we have fully understanding of great difficulties.'

'Quite. That is why we acted with the Americans and your own people.'

The Japanese had been well trained. He showed no surprise to learn, as he understood the thing, that the CIA and his own Government had been parties to the assassination of the General and that no one had told him. 'Much safety,' he said solemnly, 'in good international cooperation. Very wise action by your esteemed Government. Elimination of General Nasturtion most excellent idea.' He gestured in the direction of the Pakistani textile exporter and others in the American coffin.

The Frenchman blinked and said nothing. English as a lingua franca with a Japanese had its shortcomings.

He had no idea what the man meant. Was he suggesting the French services had sabotaged the UTA plane in order to get rid of the General? Preposterous!

Preposterous? He'd heard of odder things in his time. He resolved to send a 'most secret' cable to the Quai, pointing out tactfully that the dark secret was out. For his part, the Japanese ambassador was resolving to send a 'most secret' cable to Tokyo, stating that he had it on the authority of the French ambassador that the UTA plane had been sabotaged on the orders of the French authorities in order to dispose of the General and, presumably, get a French nominee appointed at Entakan.

He added that he had no idea as yet who the French nominee might be and in answer to his questions the French ambassador had been remarkably reticent, pleading a highly implausible ignorance. What the Frenchman had actually replied with a Gallic shrug was, 'Another of their corrupt and boneheaded army generals, I suppose. *Encore un emmerdeur.*' He was still smarting from the French failure to win the Entakan contract.

Hildegarde sat alongside the Borkh twins and the rest of the German girls. Impervious to the unintelligible oratory of the officiating mullah and the giggles of the twins, she was dreaming. In her dream she was in a castle somewhere in Scotland with her wonderful Englishman. The royal family had the castle next door and they were on visiting terms. Her children were all blonde – the girls pretty like their mother, the boys handsome like their father. They played with the royal offspring. She was finding the life of an English country lady much to her taste. She played golf, shot at different kinds of birds, gave tea parties and had a lot of fantastic sex.

Thus she mused, glancing from time to time across to where her Englishman sat, rather miserably, she thought. Perhaps he had been fond of the General and was grieving for him. Funerals were sad occasions.

She dabbed at her left eye, which seemed readier to weep than the right one. The General had been a disgusting little man, but death was death. It was always a sad affair. Her mother had taught her not to think ill of the dead.

Slowly, her mind started to grapple more seriously with the problem of the future. Would her Englishman take her back to Britain? Would he marry her? How could she help to bring such an eventuality to pass? If she had gone unbidden to the United States she could do likewise now and follow him back to London. She moved carefully, with peasant tenacity, towards her decisions. Then she shushed at the twins, whose giggles were beginning to be a noticeable feature of the proceedings.

'He'd have been no good anyway,' Sieglinde said, 'after what we did to him.'

Waldtraute nodded. 'Perhaps he's been saved from a lifetime of gut-ache.'

'Madame says we're to go to Macao from here. There's a very rich man there who pays crazy prices.'

'What colour is he?'

'She didn't say in the cable, so how should I know? He's probably a Chinese dwarf. Anyway, it can't be more boring than the General.'

They seemed only moderately interested in the new twist to their lives that the Madam from Runcorn back in Germany, had arranged for them. Like Hildegarde, they believed life to be something that happened to people, but they lacked Hildegarde's sporadic will to influence the process.

Hildegarde was right; George Pidduck was feeling apprehensive and morose. He could be on the eve of yet another commercial triumph or of the most impressive foul-up of his career. It all depended on the succession, and Mr Sombolon had assured him that no one knew who would be chosen. It had been true at the time, but events were moving at some speed and even Mr Sombolon had been left behind.

On the Government seats at the front of the assemblage, the Prime Minister and the Minister of Mines were in quiet but deep conversation.

'I received your list.'

'Did you make a choice?'

'I did.'

'Who is it to be?'

'They were all idiots or crooks.'

'I had little to choose from.' The Minister knew the value of his list, for he had constructed it with some care. Now he looked astonished and pained.

'Maybe, maybe not,' the Prime Minister said. 'Anyway, I have made my choice and the President gave in after ten minutes.'

'I am anxious to know.'

'It will be you.'

'Me?' The Minister managed a mix of reluctant astonishment designed to hide the fact that the thing was going very much his way.

'Yes, you, my friend. And there's one immediate matter the Japanese are driving me crazy about. It's this servicing contract, which I understand is now urgent.'

'Does it have to go to the Japanese?'

'Not necessarily. Why do you ask?'

'It's only that I have a good friend who represents a Brazilian company here. It's German money. A lot of German money. And they are very charming and understanding people. I'd like you to meet them.'

'And they want to tender?'

'They do. Very much. They will do anything for a trading foothold here. I would reopen the bidding to give them a chance to come in.'

'If you wish. I am not interested in the details.'

'And they particularly want to meet you. As I say, they are very understanding people.'

The Prime Minister was pensive for a moment. He listened for a while to the incantations of the mullah.

'Arrange it,' he said, 'with my secretary.'

193